Outl

Laura was surrounded by dark
corridor the floor was jagged beneath her feet but she stepped forward with a smooth stride . . . Although she was blind she had hardly been injured by the destruction of Shattershard and she walked confidently into the blackness ahead.

When Zoë finds the underground Door out of the ruined Shattershard and leads Laura, Alex, and Jhezra through it, they find themselves in a vast world of corridors leading to more corridors, and rooms lined with books. This must be the great Library that Morgan had told Zoë about—but where can they go from here? They try Door after Door, hoping to find someone to help them, to tell them where they are, and reverse the spell that had caused Laura's blindness.

Zoë is desperate to get home where her father must be going mad with worry but Laura is determined to find another world where she can use her skills to gain influence and power, just like she had in Shattershard—but this time she won't let anything—not even her lost sight—get in her way. And all the time she is thinking of a way to get her revenge on Morgan who had cast the spell that had thrust her into darkness—if she is still alive . . .

Rhiannon Lassiter was born in 1977. Her mother is also a writer and reviewed for several newspapers, ensuring that Rhiannon always had something to read. She began to read science fiction and fantasy when she was about nine years old and it is still her most enduring passion. She has always spent a lot of time reading and writing and even skipped classes at school to go to the library. The first novel she sent to a publisher wasn't accepted, but the positive feedback she received was a great boost to her confidence. Her first trilogy was published just after her nineteenth birthday, which meant combining her university degree with her writing. Rhiannon now lives in Oxford with two friends and two cats. *Outland* is the second book in her new series which also includes *Borderland* and *Shadowland*.

Also in this series:

Borderland
Shadowland

Outland

Rhiannon Lassiter

For Tony Short
who helped discover the
physics of my universe.

OXFORD
UNIVERSITY PRESS

Great Clarendon Street, Oxford OX2 6DP

Oxford University Press is a department of the University of Oxford.
It furthers the University's objective of excellence in research, scholarship,
and education by publishing worldwide in

Oxford New York
Auckland Bangkok Buenos Aires
Cape Town Chennai Dar es Salaam Delhi Hong Kong Istanbul
Karachi Kolkata Kuala Lumpur Madrid Melbourne Mexico City Mumbai
Nairobi São Paulo Shanghai Taipei Tokyo Toronto

First published 2004

British Library Cataloguing in Publication Data available

ISBN 0 19 275403 3

1 3 5 7 9 10 8 6 4 2

Typeset by AFS Image Setters Ltd, Glasgow

Printed in Great Britain by
Cox & Wyman Ltd, Reading, Berkshire

Prelude

The Hall of Echoes is a shadowy room where candlelight cannot penetrate the darkness of the great domed ceiling. Around its walls are thousands of small recesses, each large enough for a tight scroll of paper, in a honeycomb arrangement stretching high up the walls. Many of the compartments are empty, others hold their curls of paper cocooned in dusty spider's webs but on the lower levels the scrolls are fresh and new: tied with coloured ribbons or sealed with wax stamps.

In all the known worlds the Great Library is a thing apart. Inhabited solely by agents of the mysterious organization known as the Collegiate, it is said that even they do not know its true purposes or extent. Beyond this plain room lie hundreds of thousands more; all with the same book-lined walls, the same unassuming wooden furniture, the same open archways leading through more shelved corridors to more book-filled rooms. Papered with books and riddled with Doors, magical portals to other worlds, the Great Library holds more secrets than a lifetime of study could encompass.

But in the vast stacks of the Library the Hall of Echoes has its own reputation. Collegiate members are world-travellers, using the magical Doors of the Library to move from world to world before returning with journals of their travels to add to the vast catalogue of books. In their randomly weaving journeys across miles of uncharted land or between worlds in the blink of an eye these world-travellers sometimes meet. The Hall of Echoes is filled with their messages to each other. Friends, lovers, and deadly enemies come here to write their messages on the screws of paper, sealing them with their symbols and tying them with identifying ribbons or rags of fabric to await collection. Notices of rendezvous, challenges to duels, journeys end in lovers' meetings are entrusted to the honeycomb of alcoves.

Given the great height of the dome the echoes are literal as well as figurative and visitors generally walk softly and speak in lowered tones, the rustling of paper whispering quietly across the room.

'Futility.' Caravaggion's baritone voice carried easily up into the heights of the dome and floated back down to him, causing the few inhabitants of the room to look up with momentary irritation from composing their messages.

'Hush,' his companion chided gently, linking her right arm with his and drawing him towards the arched entrance of the room. 'You're disturbing people, my dear.'

'And what's wrong with disturbing people?' Caravaggion grumbled, although he permitted himself to be led out of the Hall of Echoes and along the well-lit corridor beyond the entrance. 'You grow entirely too complacent, Lisle. The air here is stale.'

Lisle Weft's lips twitched at that. The air in this corridor, as in all of the Great Library, was still and close; lightly dusted with the smell of books and ink.

'Let's go to my study,' she said, reaching down to pat the rough head of the russet-coloured dog that walked patiently at her heel. 'You can tell me whatever's on your mind there.'

'On my mind?' Caravaggion repeated with a hint of irritation. 'Lisle, this is more than some personal dissatisfaction, this is serious, this is . . .'

'A matter of life and death?' Lisle's mouth twisted wryly. 'Yes, I know. You said as much in your message.'

'I never thanked you for coming,' Caravaggion remembered belatedly. 'Forgive me, I am grateful, I didn't expect you so soon.'

'As it happens it was no trouble. I've been spending some time in this section myself recently,' Lisle said slowly. 'In fact I'm now a member of the Jurist faction.'

'You are?' Caravaggion glanced at her in sudden surprise. 'I mean I knew you could often be found here but I didn't realize your ties with the Jurists were that close. Did you say you had a study here?'

'Yes I have.' Lisle quirked a smile at him. 'And I have wine and food there and even a censer to sweeten the stale air.'

'Very well,' Caravaggion said with a reluctant smile, his dark mood beginning to subside in the face of her relentless patience. 'Which way?'

As they walked down the curving corridor Lisle's dog kept pace with them, ears pricking to attention whenever another world-traveller passed by. The Jurist section was always busy and other Collegiate members stopped to exchange a word or nod of greeting with Lisle or spare Caravaggion a curious glance as they passed by.

Caravaggion himself watched Lisle. Her iron-grey hair

was waist-length, instead of the bushy mop he remembered from his last visit to Jurist territory, and plaited neatly down her back. Her face was a little more lined and her walk just a little slower as well but other than that she was the same Lisle Weft she had always been. Her comfortable uniform of trousers and a woollen tunic was as familiar to him as the presence of a dog following behind her. She had had a whole pack of them once, he remembered, drawing her carriage across a green valley on her home world when she came to meet him at the Door. Her attitude to them, as always, had been one of uncompromising affection. Now it struck him that she was the same way with men.

They'd been friends once, long ago and far away from here. They'd been antagonists as well, sometimes disagreeing so violently that they'd refused to speak for months or even years. But none of that was as important to Caravaggion as the fact that Lisle was someone who understood; she might disagree with many of his opinions but she never dismissed them and he had always tried to accord her the same respect.

It wasn't until they were established in comfortable leather chairs in Lisle's study that they resumed their earlier conversation. Caravaggion stretched out his hands to the warmth of the cheerful fire burning in a low brazier set at one side of the room at a safe distance away from the heaps of books and paper; Lisle placed a dish of water on the floor for her dog and poured out two glasses of a rich ruby wine.

'You seem to live well here at least,' Caravaggion said, striving for lightness in his tone.

'It's not as luxurious as some sections I've seen but it serves,' Lisle said dismissively. 'But I'm not here all the time. I still have family on Fenrisnacht.'

'Yes, I remember.' Caravaggion raised his glass to her

slightly before taking a sip of his wine. 'How are your children?'

'Grandchildren now too,' Lisle told him. 'Meaga is holding the fort and having a baby every other year; Lechto's moved out to the marchings with his wife and she's had her first already; and Siffany's still in the army and away at court most of the time.'

'It all sounds very comfortable and domestic,' Caravaggion said and Lisle glared at him.

'You know well it isn't,' she said. 'Just as you know at what cost we've gained the peace we have.' The russet-brindled dog raised its head at the snap of annoyance in Lisle's voice and emitted a low whine which drew its owner to look at it. 'It's all right, Pepper,' she said in a gentler voice and then, with a tone of command: 'Down, red dog. There now.'

'He's new, isn't he?' Caravaggion said, noticing the dog properly for the first time. 'Wasn't the last one more yellowish?'

'Mustard,' his companion agreed. 'She got too tired to keep up, poor old girl. This young fellow's only been with me for a few months. I think he misses the fresh air.'

'Mmm,' said Caravaggion noncommittally.

He watched as Lisle scratched behind the dog's pointed ears and tried to think of something conciliatory to say. But it was Lisle who was the first to speak again.

'Come now,' she said, with a wry look. 'Let's not rehash old arguments. Tell me why you've come to visit me here and what it is that troubles you.'

'It's a long story,' Caravaggion began and at Lisle's twitch of a smile he laughed ruefully and added: 'I know it always is . . . but this goes back many years to the beginning of my search.'

'This quest for the Founders of the Library.' Lisle shook her head in a gesture of weariness. 'You've been looking for them all your life and are still no further on than when you began . . .'

'No one knows it better than I,' Caravaggion admitted. 'But my wanderings have led me to some interesting places even if I haven't found the answers I've looked for.' He paused. 'Besides, I wouldn't say I'm no further on. There are things I've learnt about the Library itself that have led to some interesting conclusions, especially tracing back the evolution of the current factions. I'm currently following up a lead on one of the ancient Legends. Have you heard of the worlds of light?'

'It's an ancient magic myth, isn't it? A race of magicians who left artefacts of power out in the worlds.'

'It's more than that. I've seen some of the items supposedly made by them in Artificer territory and they are far beyond magic. The Artificers have been collecting them for a while now and they've had to evolve an entirely new glyphographical system for explaining how they function. It goes to the root of why magic differs so dramatically across different worlds.'

'Indeed.' Lisle took another sip from her wine and Caravaggion raised his eyebrows at her.

'You might not see the importance yourself, Lisle. But trust me, this could be crucial. However, this is by the by. The point is that I've been spending time with the Artificers recently and making short travels in and around the Mandela.'

'You're now based on your home world then?' Lisle asked and Caravaggion raised his glass to her.

'As you are,' he said drily. 'Such old adventurers we are. We travelled so far in our day and yet we both have come home in the end.'

'After so long an absence you never really go home,' Lisle said slowly, reaching down to stroke the silky head of the red dog. 'But go on . . . the Mandela.'

'The Mandela was, of course, where my quest began. If I hadn't grown up in Mandarel I would probably have lived my whole life on the same world.'

Lisle almost choked on her wine as she started laughing and Caravaggion's face went through several expressions of affront, concern, impatience, and finally reluctant amusement as she laughed herself out of breath and eventually subsided.

'You live on one world?' she said when she'd finally recovered herself. 'You're a wanderer by nature, Caravaggion. If you ever do find the Founders I expect you'll discover they made the Doors and the Library to satisfy your unquenchable appetite for new discoveries.'

'Point taken,' Caravaggion admitted, and Lisle gestured towards the wine bottle with a more conciliatory air.

'Have some more,' she said. 'There are ginger wafers in the box on the table if you'd like some.' She waited while he inspected the contents of a green jade box before going on. 'I take your point though that the Mandela is unique.'

'Well, it's an ancient city in itself and its own records rival any Library section.' Caravaggion nodded, picking up the train of his argument. 'And it's got one of the best-mapped networks of Doors because so many people start from there or reach it eventually. But because of its location in Library terms it's a working city rather than a scholarly one so it takes a while for certain pieces of more esoteric information to filter back.'

'Now we come to it.' Lisle's eyes narrowed, displaying more curiosity than she had up until this point. 'You know,' she added with affected lightness in her tone, 'Lachesis once said that you were the best spymaster she ever had. I suppose that's one part of your quest for knowledge you'd not be so willing to admit to.'

'Oh, I'd willingly admit it,' Caravaggion said quickly.

'Why, are you planning to hold me on trial in your Converse Court?'

'Not I.' Lisle shook her head. 'Though not all the Jurists are disposed to love you, Caravaggion.'

'Their minds are as stale as the air in this section,' Caravaggion said sharply. 'I'm surprised to find you working for them, Lisle.'

'I have my reasons,' she said with dignity and he frowned.

'Or you think you do,' he said. 'Seriously, do you think the Jurists are doing much good for the Library?'

'They bring people together in this section of the Library,' Lisle said. 'They . . . I mean we . . . ' She paused. 'Look, I'll be honest with you. They're the most influential group in this area of the Library and completely law abiding. I was able to arrange a study here and once you're based in any area you tend to get affiliated with it sooner or later. It's not the first faction I've belonged to and it won't be the last.'

Caravaggion took a draught of his wine, arranging his thoughts, and Lisle waited patiently for him to go on.

'I wouldn't be too sure about that,' he said. 'I've heard rumours . . . you know how difficult it is to work out connections in the Library, but as far as I can tell the rumours tend in this direction.'

'I have no idea what you're talking about,' Lisle said frankly. 'But do go on.'

'Forgive me.' Caravaggion was betrayed into a laugh. 'Well, the truth of it is that I've heard rumours of undue influence, of worlds being brought under the control of some power-broker faction in a very subtle and insidious way.'

'Indeed?' Lisle looked thoughtful for a moment and then she narrowed her eyes at him. 'And this is supposed to be happening somewhere near to the Jurist section?'

'No,' Caravaggion said definitely. 'They come from distant worlds and obscure connections. They suggest that a powerful faction is expanding through a series of worlds, influencing the governments and controlling the access through all their Doors.'

'Ridiculous,' Lisle said. 'The Library is large but I've heard nothing of any such thing for decades. Not since the atrocities of the Gleaners has any such control been attempted by any faction. If something like that was going on, we'd have heard of it.'

'Not necessarily.' Caravaggion shook his head. 'And in any case the rumours suggest this faction has powerful forces on its side, soldiers and probably strong mages as well. They sweep everything before them. Quite literally.'

'Well, if it's so what has it got to do with us?' Lisle asked.

'Little is known about the leaders of this faction,' Caravaggion said. 'I have only been able to piece together its existence from scattered rumours and suggestions. But they or their agents use a faction device. A disc symbol with red and black markings.' Lisle frowned and Caravaggion leant forward. 'And,' he concluded, 'there's a faction called the Wheel with a territory near the edge of Jurist influence that uses a symbol very like what I've described.'

Lisle lay back in her chair thinking for a moment, before suddenly reaching for a small notebook on a nearby table. Flicking through it quickly she paused a couple of times to read something before dropping the book in her lap.

'There is a faction called the Wheel,' she said. 'I remember them now. A group of their members have come through here twice. Once travelling somewhere at speed, once trading for books and listening to the lectures in the Converse Court. They were very formal and very polite.

They did wear a device in those colours though.' Her brows knit together as she thought again. 'How convinced are you that this Wheel is involved in illegal influence?'

'If they are the faction I believe them to be it goes beyond influence,' Caravaggion said grimly. 'Oh, they show the velvet glove approach in general. They prefer subtlety and conspiracy over overt control, but when someone opposes their aims they are ruthless. They'll stoop to murder or torture if it suits their ends.'

'If this is true they must be challenged,' Lisle exclaimed and her companion gave her a long look.

'If this is true they are more powerful than the Jurists,' he said patiently. 'This goes beyond your Court's kind of arbitration and they'll not submit to your decisions.'

'What then?' Lisle asked sharply. 'Why come with these suspicions if you don't want them acted upon?'

'If the Jurists were better able to defend their position I'd argue otherwise,' he told her. 'But they're bogged down between cultists and collectors and cranks. No one here's really equipped to handle a serious threat. We're a long way away from the Lightbringers now.'

'A long way and a long time.' Lisle stared into the glow of the brazier, through the flickering flames. 'I'm old now. Too old for drama.'

'The Library is old,' Caravaggion said distractedly. 'Don't be maudlin, Lisle, it's not that long since those days of adventure of yours. You said you were old when you fought beside the Lightbringers but you won just the same.'

'Well, if I was old then I'm older still now,' Lisle said but her eyes sparkled in the fire's leaping light. 'I'm not about to pick up a sword again, my hands have held a pen for too long. If violence erupts in the Library I'll be off to Fenrisnacht.'

'Fair enough.' Caravaggion looked down at his own

hands, calloused and ink stained, each finger banded with several metal rings. 'All I want is for you to watch and be wary. Danger tends to come suddenly and from the direction you least expect it.'

'And what about the other Jurists?' Lisle asked. 'Have you talked to anyone else about these premonitions of yours?'

'Those who will listen,' he said drily. 'But your faction has grown too certain of itself and flagrant breaches of its own code go unnoticed amidst a host of petty details. Those I know from old engagements have let themselves stultify here for too long. Persiflage Demosthene thinks only of barter and bargains, Dalandran the Itinerant dreams and does nothing, Sibilant Askew agrees with me but with her support I'm more hampered than helped. Visitors to this section are caught up in their own affairs. They will not heed my warnings.'

Lisle was silent, sipping slowly at her glass of wine. This time she did not protest at his judgement of her faction as grown stale. Compared to Caravaggion's own enthusiasm it was true. In all his life he had seemingly never grown tired of searching for an explanation of the Library's existence or the source of the magic that had created the Doors.

'You've been right before, I know,' she said. 'Great events have come about from no more than your sense of restlessness. You've always been my barometer when the weather changes.'

'Thank you.' Caravaggion bowed his head. 'Then, in that case, I will take my leave of you.'

'What will you do?' she asked. 'While I'm watching and being wary?'

'I'll speak one last time in the Converse Court,' Caravaggion said with a sigh. 'Although I doubt that many will listen. Then I return to Mandarel to follow up my own quest. But if I come across anything more concrete about these rumours or the Wheel I'll try to send word.'

'Very well.'

Lisle pushed herself to her feet and went with him to the entrance of her study, the red dog padding across to her side as she watched Caravaggion walk away down the corridor. She patted Pepper absent-mindedly. Old friends or old antagonists, it was always strange to watch them leave for a trip across worlds not knowing how many years or worlds distant your next encounter would be.

'Still walking the long road,' she said quietly to the dog. 'Perhaps you'd like to be out there with him.' The dog whined and she ruffled its ears gently. 'Or maybe you'd just like to go home.'

1

The evening sky glowed crimson and gold behind her as Morgan sat on the edge of the garden fountain. A light breeze riffled the water, wavering her reflection as she stared down into the small round pool, and sparkled the rippling water with sunlight. It was a warm summer evening and the garden was quiet with the lazy hum of insects and scattered chirruping bird calls. A little while ago two servant girls had come out of the inn behind her but when they'd seen Morgan sitting by the fountain they had stopped talking and gone quietly through an arch to the herb garden.

Watching her reflection re-form on the surface of the water, Morgan could guess why they'd left her alone and she saw the smile spread slowly across her face like the Cheshire Cat's grin. Dressed in scruffy black clothes with her hair matted into a long untidy black plait and her face grimy with three days of road dust, she didn't feel as if she looked at all remarkable. But this was a different world.

Once Morgan had been an ordinary schoolgirl, lonely and miserable. That had ended when she'd found a Door Between Worlds and begun a second secret life in the desert city of Shattershard. Now Shattershard was destroyed and she had turned her back on the Door back to Earth to come through the mountains to this peaceful green valley.

Wetting her hands in the water, Morgan wiped them across her face, trying to rub the grit away from her eyes. Somewhere inside the inn her companions would be arranging rooms and board but she'd felt the need to be on her own for a little while. It wasn't all that long ago that she'd been alone most of the time and she was surprised to find that she almost missed it. Not enough to want to go back to the way she was before but enough to make her realize that she felt uneasy with herself. In all the stories she'd read about magical worlds, the characters had ended up coming back to Earth. Morgan wondered what it said about you not to go back when your adventure was over.

Looking back down at her reflection captured in the bowl of the fountain Morgan tried to see herself the way she was in this world. Here she was a mage and Collegiate member, part of the secret organization of world-travellers. She had powerful friends and a prince as her lover, whom she'd rescued from the collapse of Shattershard. She was a powerful and dangerous person, someone to be reckoned with. Morgan tried another smile and saw it still on her face as she stared through the flat water at the grey stone floor of the pool below. Brushing her hands through the water she erased the overlapping images in a flurry of ripples and bent her head.

People had died in Shattershard. People that Kal, her prince, had felt responsible for and people he'd known all his life had died in that final battle. Morgan had left her old life behind because she'd wanted to. Kal hadn't had that choice. Everything he used to be had been left behind in Shattershard, buried under thousands of tonnes of broken rock, except the crown he'd still been wearing when the city fell in.

Crouched on the side of the fountain, Morgan looked down at her hands, still wet with the water from the fountain, and wiped them on her tunic. They were her own hands, pale-skinned with ragged fingernails and blisters from the reins of the pony. But she'd seen a blast of black fire come from these same hands, called up by her rage and fury, to envelope her enemy in a cloud of darkness. She'd never intended to use magic to hurt someone, never considered the possibility, caught up in the wonder that magic even existed in this world. But she'd used her power against Laura and she didn't even know if she regretted it.

Laura and Alex Harrell had engineered the collapse of Shattershard. Alex had done it for glory, caught up in his own fantasy of leading a desert army to victory. Morgan still didn't understand why Laura had done it. She'd never understood Laura back in Weybridge when the other girl had been a star student who breezed confidently through life. But in Shattershard Laura had become a spy and a manipulator, careless of the consequences as she pulled strings to gain power. Laura and Alex were probably dead by now and with them the desert nomads they'd used in their plan. And also with them had been Zoë but that wasn't something Morgan wanted to think about at all.

A shadow crossed over her shoulder, darkening the water and abruptly reflecting the reddened light of sunset in the pool. Morgan sat up as a familiar figure sat down beside her and she saw Kal's reflection join hers in the fountain.

'Did you want to be alone?' Kal asked as she turned to look at him and Morgan shook her head slightly, reaching out instinctively as he took her hand. 'The twins have bespoken two rooms and ordered a meal,' Kal said, lacing his fingers with hers. 'They said we should talk later if you weren't too tired.'

'I'm not too tired,' Morgan said. 'How are you feeling?'

Kal smiled with half his mouth and lifted his free hand in an empty gesture. They'd been asking each other variations of that question during the passage through the mountains and it didn't get any easier to answer. She'd felt grateful for the tough schedule the twins had set which left them too tired by the time they set up camp to do much more than eat and sleep. It wasn't surprising that now they had time they would have to talk properly for once.

Looking at Kal, his golden hair meshed with the silvery circuit of the Archon's crown and his grey eyes bruised by shadows, Morgan thought to herself that he still seemed like a prince. It was impossible to imagine him as anything else, as a sixth-former at school back on Earth or even as a normal young man on this world. There was something about Kal that made it impossible to forget that he had been brought up to rule from the moment he was born. But instead of being a barrier between them Morgan found it made it easier for her to be with him. With Kal she felt more like the person she wanted to be.

'What will you do now?' she asked softly and Kal tilted his head at her.

'Me? I'd rather know what you're intending to do,' he told her and Morgan frowned. 'I still hardly know anything about you,' Kal reminded her. 'Or about where you come from.'

'Where I come from.' Morgan shook her head. 'It isn't important . . . because I'm never going back. But where we go next . . . ' Her voice trailed off. 'I suppose the twins might have some ideas about that.'

'I'm certain they do,' Kal said levelly. 'But I know them even less well than I know you and I don't feel as inclined for their company.'

Morgan glanced up at that and caught Kal regarding her thoughtfully. Dropping her hand he reached out and brushed his thumb across her cheek gently.

'You saved my life,' he said. 'And I'm trying to learn to be grateful for that. But you and the twins obviously have your own plans. So I have to wonder if I'm a part of them.'

Morgan bit her lips, wondering what Kal was trying to say and what the right reply would be. The twins had told her that Collegiate members weren't supposed to tell anyone about the existence of Doors Between Worlds and so she'd kept silent on the subject. But the destruction of Shattershard had come about because of world-travellers trying to take over the city and maybe if she hadn't been silent then she could have stopped it. The Collegiate's rules could wait, Morgan decided; she couldn't have a relationship with someone and not tell him the truth.

'I've never had a plan,' she said slowly, looking at the pale evening sky reflected in the water. 'All I ever wanted was to be special.'

'You are special,' Kal said, getting the smile right this time, and Morgan met his eyes at last.

'Perhaps,' she said eventually. 'But this is a different world.'

Laura was surrounded by darkness. As she walked down the corridor the floor was jagged beneath her feet but she stepped forward with a smooth stride, allowing herself to be guided by the hand that supported her arm. Although she was blind she had hardly been injured by the destruction of Shattershard and she walked confidently into the blackness ahead.

On her right Zoë's footsteps trod a carefully measured stride. She hadn't spoken for hours, except to warn Laura of obstructions or turnings, and her hand had dampened the sleeve of Laura's dress with sweat. They had been wandering for three days and Zoë had led the way all that time, supporting Laura for every step, making the decisions about which path they would take ever since they'd been trapped underneath the collapsing mountain.

It had been Zoë who, against all the odds, had found the Door beneath the city. Laura hadn't believed it was possible but Zoë had insisted the Door existed and that it was their only hope of survival.

'Either we try and find this Door or we can curl up and die here,' she'd said, demanding for the first time that the others follow her lead. 'Which choice do *you* prefer?'

Jhezra and Alex had agreed to follow Zoë and now they brought up the rear of the group, their feet ringing out in an uncertain rhythm as they made their way along together. They'd both been injured but how badly Laura didn't know and she couldn't tell if it was Alex supporting Jhezra or the other way around.

When Zoë had stumbled into the Door beneath the mountain she'd thought they were saved. Dropping Laura's arm in her excitement she'd exclaimed suddenly, rushing forward and scrambling down what sounded like a shifting slide of scattered rock. Ominous rumblings from the cavern ceiling boomed above them as Zoë's scrambles sent a lighter scatter of pebbles bouncing and cracking across the floor.

'Thanks be to all the gods,' Jhezra had exclaimed as Zoë's voice called back the news of her discovery. 'We must hurry. I fear this area is becoming unstable.'

She and Alex had set off down the rock scree leaving Laura to wait until Zoë came back for her and helped her down the shifting mass of fallen stone.

'This is it,' Zoë had told her when they reached the Door. 'I haven't been through yet. We still don't know what's on the other side.'

'Whatever it is has got to be better than this,' Alex had said and Laura felt Zoë's hand clench on her arm.

'Let's go then,' Zoë had said curtly, pulling Laura onwards, and in a single step the rumblings of the mountain and the damp air of the caves had been replaced by a sudden warmth and the musty smell of dust and books. The others had gasped with relief but later they'd come to admit what Laura had realized from the first: finding the Door hadn't helped.

Admittedly they were no longer in danger of being crushed to death. But without water or food their situation wasn't much improved. The book-filled room on the other side of the Door had led into a book-lined corridor and from there into a maze of more rooms and corridors, through which Zoë had led them with slowly diminishing confidence.

'Morgan said something about a Library,' she'd told them. 'I think this must be it.'

They'd stopped more than once to take down books from the shelves. Jhezra hadn't been able to read them but Alex and Zoë both wore magical charms for translation and had scanned through them quickly.

'It's impossible,' Alex had said when they finally abandoned the books. 'I can't work out half of what these are about and when I can . . . ' his voice died away.

'There's nothing useful to us,' Zoë confirmed. 'I can't even work out if they're fact or fiction. They're about places and things I've never heard of. Nothing about where we are or anything that explains what this is a Library for.'

'There are signs though,' Jhezra told them. 'Marks on

the shelves or on the floor. Like trail marks.' But neither Alex or Zoë had been able to understand what the signs meant.

'We'll have to go on,' Zoë decided. 'Sooner or later we're bound to find someone who we can ask for help.'

They hadn't. In over two days of wandering they'd found endless rooms and corridors of books but not a single other person. What they had found were Doors. Zoë had noticed the first but before they could discuss whether to go through it Jhezra had spotted another. Making a rough camp of their belongings they'd left Laura standing beside it as they explored a couple of nearby corridors and came back with the news that there were Doors everywhere dotted up and down the branching corridors of the Library.

'This is really strange,' Alex said. 'How can there be so many?'

'Are many more strange than one?' Jhezra asked and Laura heard an odd note in her voice.

'It is strange though,' Zoë had replied. 'It's . . . it's so far away from normal I don't even know what to think of it.'

'Then maybe we should try one of the Doors,' Laura had suggested patiently and for a moment silence answered her before Zoë said suddenly:

'No.'

'There might be food or water on the other side,' Jhezra had said, pointing out the obvious, but Zoë remained intransigent.

'There might be anything on the other side,' she said. 'I don't think it's safe to look. Or even right for us to try. We should keep exploring this place.'

'As you wish.' Jhezra had accepted Zoë's decision without argument, the same way she'd accepted Zoë's lead from the beginning. Alex had tried several more times to persuade her but without any support had given up. Laura had stayed silent. She was still making up her mind what she thought about Zoë.

Back on Earth Zoë hadn't been anyone important. She'd changed schools half a dozen times before her father's army job had brought her to Weybridge and she had kept a low profile in the hope of fitting in. It wasn't until half term that Laura had noticed anything interesting about Zoë but when she did she had decided to take the other girl with her through the Door into Shattershard.

'She could be useful,' Laura had insisted when Alex objected to bringing Zoë in on their secret world, not giving her reasons for why she thought so.

Alex had caved in as he always did: more interested in playing Alexander the Conqueror in battle than in the fine details of society politics. If she was honest with herself Laura hadn't had any idea what Zoë might be useful for except that it would have been a waste to leave behind someone so obviously impressed by her. She'd thought of the red-headed girl as a follower and her instincts had served her well given that now she was blind and required Zoë's help even to walk. But unfortunately Zoë seemed to think that *she* was the leader now and that didn't suit Laura at all.

But blind and weaponless, owning only the clothes she wore and a few valuable items she'd saved from Shattershard, without even the merest of clues to where they were, there was no point in Laura attempting to assert herself. Instead she listened to the sound of weary footsteps and the scattered phrases that passed between the others. Earth and the world of the Tetrarchate were behind her now and Laura's pale green eyes looked down the corridor ahead towards a future she couldn't see.

* * *

From an upstairs window of the tavern Charm looked down at the two figures sitting together at the edge of the fountain. A gentle smile curved her lips as she watched them for a moment longer before turning away.

'Why were you smiling?' her twin asked from across the room. And Charm looked over at him, her expression becoming grave again.

'Morgan intends to tell Kal about the Collegiate,' she said. 'She believes that her love for him requires it.'

'Did you expect anything else?' Ciren asked and Charm frowned.

'We told her not to,' she reminded him. 'And Kal is a complication.'

Ciren was silent for a while as he thought and Charm reached out to finish closing the shutters and drew a thin muslin curtain across the window. Ciren watched her and wondered what she was thinking. It wasn't a thing he'd ever had cause to wonder about before. The twins had lived their lives as one single unit so much that he'd come to believe that they thought and felt as one person as well. But this last mission to Shattershard had changed something. Kal's crown, which made him immune to Charm's mind-reading ability, had set him thinking properly about his twin's unusual power. Now, having seen her casually reading Morgan's mind with no thought to her privacy, he felt suddenly uncomfortable with his other half.

'It's the most broken of all the Collegiate rules,' he said, after a while. 'Across all the factions. Everyone does it sooner or later for whatever reason. And she loves him.'

'The Wheel might not be pleased,' she said. 'Morgan could make a good agent if she comes back to the Great Library with us. But if she wants to bring Kal with her there might be problems.'

'Perhaps not too many,' Ciren pointed out. 'He has

nothing tying him here. His city tried to be independent of the Tetrarchate; now that it's gone he has no place in this world. And if Morgan brings him through to the Great Library he will be a world-traveller and there's no reason why the Wheel shouldn't consider him as great an asset as Morgan.'

'How can we know that?' Charm asked. 'I can't read him. We still don't know what he's like.'

Ciren frowned, wondering what to say first. He would have liked to point out that Kal had survived the destruction of Shattershard better than he had expected. The boy Archon who'd been powerless to prevent the disaster had settled into a grim-eyed refugee who held himself together through strength of will alone. But more than that he wanted to explain to Charm that there were more ways to assess people than riffling through their minds.

'Why do you look like that?' Charm asked suddenly. She wasn't smiling and her violet eyes were hard and black. 'I don't know what it means when you look at me like that.'

Ciren hesitated and then shook his head.

'It's the crown,' he said. 'It's throwing us off. I keep wondering about what it means that you can't read him. It's started me thinking about possibilities . . . ' he shook his head. 'I'm still not certain what they mean.'

'It makes me wonder as well,' Charm told him, her stance relaxing at his explanation. 'No one's been able to block me before. I didn't think it was possible.'

Ciren nodded, relieved that the discussion had moved away from uncomfortable thoughts about how his twin read people.

'It's also not typical of other magics we've encountered in this world,' he said. 'The enchantments on that crown are unusually complex. I wonder what its history is.'

'Perhaps we can persuade Kal to tell us,' Charm suggested.

'Perhaps,' Ciren agreed, without trying to analyse what she meant by persuade. 'But it's possible he doesn't even know its properties or provenance. And if he doesn't know that it can block you . . . '

'There's no need to make him a present of the information,' Charm agreed, finishing his thought and putting them in sync with each other again.

Laura's cough sounded drily in the long corridor for a third time and Jhezra tensed at the noise. Beside her Alex kept walking onwards drearily; once more in a daze of depression at their situation. He didn't even seem to notice when Jhezra tried to talk to him and showed no more interest in the dry hacking noise of Laura's coughing fit.

Up ahead Zoë had come to a halt, keeping her arm around Laura as she asked if she was all right. Jhezra stopped walking and tapped her companion lightly on the arm.

'Alexander,' she said. 'Stop for a moment.'

His feet shuffled on for another few paces before her message penetrated and then he stood still and blinked for a moment.

'What . . . ' he began and Jhezra moistened her lips while she remembered that impatience solves nothing.

'Laura is unwell,' she said levelly. 'We should stop while Zoë attends to her.'

Alex nodded, slumping down on the floor obediently and rubbing at the improvised bandage around his right arm. Jhezra didn't sit beside him though. It annoyed her that Alex hadn't realized that she was no longer using the version of his name he had first given her. Back in the desert outside Shattershard he'd told her his name was

Iskander. It wasn't a complete lie but a pronunciation of his name which had also been used for his hero: Alexander of Macedon. All the same Jhezra was no longer comfortable calling him by it and she wondered why he hadn't noticed the change.

Laura's hacking coughs eventually came to an end and Jhezra glanced up at Zoë, who was frowning at Laura. Early on in their travels she'd torn a strip of cloth from her shirt to tie over Laura's blind and staring eyes but Jhezra felt as if she could still see that blank gaze through the folded bandage.

'All right,' Zoë said softly, although no one had spoken to her. 'I suppose we're going to have to try one of the Doors.'

'We need water,' Jhezra agreed, trying not to let it sound like a criticism. She looked over at Laura standing silently beside them and then at the slumped figure of Alex on the floor of the corridor. 'Food is less important but we cannot manage much longer without water.'

'I've been saying that for ages,' Alex said petulantly, lifting his head. 'This place is deserted. We have to use a Door.'

'I know.' Zoë stared at the floor. 'I was hoping it wouldn't come to this though.' She looked up again and directly at Jhezra, meeting her eyes seriously. 'We have no idea what kind of world might be on the other side of any of these Doors,' she said. 'It could be dangerous for us there. Also . . . we could be dangerous for it.'

'Dangerous?' Laura's laugh sounded much more lightly than her cough had. 'A band of cripples with one weapon between us? What danger could we possibly be?'

'Well, seeing as the last time you went through a Door you ended up destroying a city and killing God only knows how many people in the process, I don't think you have a leg to stand on, Laura.' Zoë's eyes flashed at her erstwhile friend for an instant before she shook her head suddenly as if shaking away her anger. 'But I admit we have no choice.'

Jhezra said nothing, feeling bad for Zoë but not knowing how to help. She wanted to be able to talk to the red-headed girl better, to speak her language without the aid of the translation charm, to explain that she didn't blame Zoë for what had happened. She didn't even blame Alex and Laura as much as herself. Without Jhezra's suggestion the Hajhim would never have listened to Alex's ideas for taking over Shattershard and the destruction of the fortress city would never have taken place. But Zoë, with much less reason, also felt responsible. Jhezra knew that as certainly as if Zoë had shouted it in her ear but she wouldn't speak of these things in front of Laura and Alex. Instead she started looking for a suitable Door.

When Morgan had finished her story, Kal sat for a while in silence still holding her hand in a firm grip. His head was bent as he tried to assimilate everything she had told him and Morgan watched him with concern in her eyes.

'So this Laura and Alex are responsible for the Hajhim attacking Shattershard,' he said finally in a low voice.

'They were trading with the Hajhim for ages,' Morgan admitted. 'I warned Laura over and over again that she didn't have any right to interfere. And Alex had a lover among the Hajhim. I knew they were planning something but I didn't know what.' She shivered a little in the night air as she fixed Kal with a pleading look. 'I'm sorry I didn't tell you this before. I feel so guilty . . . '

'I'm sorry too,' Kal said, meeting her eyes. 'If I'd known.' His eyes were hard for a moment then he shook his head. 'No, we can talk about that later. What I want to know now is about Ciren and Charm. You said they belonged to an organization of world-travellers?'

'I wasn't supposed to tell you,' Morgan said, tightening her hold on Kal's hand. 'But I had to. I couldn't keep something like this from you . . . I never will again, I promise. Please, you have to believe that!' Her voice shook a bit on the words and she stopped speaking, trying to get control of her voice.

'I understand,' Kal said and he put an arm around her. 'I do appreciate your honesty. But I need to know more. If the twins are world-travellers why didn't they stop these other people, Laura and Alex, why didn't they stop them from destroying my city?'

Morgan huddled closer to Kal in the circle of his arm. The sun had set over the garden and the stone rim of the fountain was cold and uncomfortable but Kal seemed not to notice, half in a daze with what she was saying.

'They wanted to stop it,' Morgan explained. 'The Collegiate has rules about not interfering with other worlds or bringing through weapons to dominate them. We were going to find Laura and Alex and talk to them but . . . I left it too late. It took me a while to believe the twins and by the time I did . . . the battle had already begun.' Her eyes felt wet and she hid her head against Kal's shoulder and whispered: 'I'm sorry.'

'I know.' Kal stroked a hand down Morgan's hair and she felt him sigh. Then he spoke with a sudden bitterness that made her wince. 'I hope I killed him,' he said. 'It was Alex I fought at the palace gate, wasn't it? But even if I didn't the city did. I don't see how he could have made it out alive.'

'No, I don't see how,' Morgan agreed.

Her mind shifted away from the thought of Zoë. She'd barely mentioned Zoë in her story, still unsure of her feelings about the red-headed girl she hardly knew, but it was Zoë she'd tried to save. If Zoë had found her way to the Door beneath the city it was possible that she might have escaped. But in her heart Morgan felt certain that Zoë was dead, and Laura and Alex with her, entombed beneath the broken city of Shattershard.

'So he's dead,' Kal said again with a curiously unsatisfied note in his voice and Morgan glanced up at him.

'And Laura too,' she added. 'I cast a spell . . . I'm still not sure what I did . . . But I think it might have killed her. It looked . . . ' She shook her head, not wanting to remember the black cloud that had enveloped Laura, but Kal looked suddenly less cold.

'You took our side,' he said softly. 'I still remember you joining us on the battlements. You and Edren and Athen.' He stroked Morgan's hair again. 'I still miss them,' he said quietly. 'But at least I have you even if everything else is gone.'

'There's you,' Morgan said, groping for words. 'You're still alive. You're still the Archon . . . ' She stopped when she saw him wince.

'No, all that is gone now,' Kal said with an air of finality and he shifted a bit on the stone seat. 'Come on,' he said, drawing Morgan to her feet. 'Let's go inside. You must be freezing.'

'I'm all right,' Morgan said automatically, but she leant into Kal's arms as he rubbed her shoulders to warm her up.

'We've both left our old lives behind now,' Kal said thoughtfully as they walked back towards the inn. 'This world has nothing left for me. Lead on, wherever you wish, Morgan, I have nowhere else to be but with you.'

As they reached the kitchen door Kal let Morgan through first and hung back for one last moment to shut the door behind him. The inn was golden with warmth and the smell of freshly baked bread as he followed Morgan across the room to join the twins by the side of a fiercely crackling fire.

2

Darkness flashed and Zoë stepped through the Door. Jhezra was waiting on the other side already, biding her time as Zoë led Laura through and Alex followed after them. Scouting ahead, Jhezra had already described what she'd seen here since this was their third attempt at trying a Door. The first had opened out on a bleak hillside with no sign of water anywhere near and the second had been a dark jungle smelling of rot and animal droppings. This time Jhezra had come back eagerly, urging them to join her here.

It was light on this side and the sun shone palely in a cloudy grey sky. They stood in a clearing among low trees on a white platform of stone: on one side was the Door set perfectly in an oval arch of plain stone and on the other a raised stone basin held a bowl of water. On the edge of the basin was a brown ceramic cup.

Jhezra had waited for them before drinking and now she filled the cup from the basin and sipped cautiously while the others watched.

'Tastes sweet,' she said. 'But like water. I think it is safe to drink.' She paused for a longer draught of the liquid and then offered the cup to Zoë. 'But do not drink too fast,' she warned. 'Even good water could make us sick after so long without it.'

Zoë took a sip, feeling the cool water slide down her aching throat like tears, and took a long breath of relief. Then she helped guide the cup into Laura's waiting hands, while Alex crossed to the basin and imitated Jhezra in scooping up handfuls of the water.

'See, I knew we'd find something if we tried a Door,' Alex told her and Zoë winced at the note of triumph in his voice.

Instead of answering she drank some more water. But as she looked down into the basin she felt a pang as she saw the clear water now clouded slightly with dust. She rubbed her wet hands over her face to feel the coolness of them before wiping them carefully on her shirt.

'Don't get the water dirty,' she said more sharply than she'd intended and turned to refill the cup for Laura.

Jhezra nodded at her across Alex's head and took a step down from the stone platform to wipe her hands on the close-cropped grass.

'This was placed for us,' she said to Zoë, turning back to gesture at the archway with the Door. 'Whoever lives in this place knows of this Door and has prepared this water bowl in readiness for those who cross through.' Suddenly she looked up into the sky and made a lifting gesture with her hands holding them up to the sunshine. 'May the gods smile upon the people of this place,' she called out. 'For they are kind to weary travellers.'

No one answered her but Zoë abruptly felt better and she left Laura with the water cup and went to join Jhezra on the grass.

'Do you think that's fruit?' she asked softly, looking at

the ring of small trees that surrounded them. Here and there on the branches were dotted small yellow globes.

'Such kindness,' Jhezra said, her voice full of wonder, and she smiled suddenly at Zoë showing her straight white teeth. 'I feel sure the fruit will be good to eat. I feel as if I know these people already.'

With such certainty from Jhezra, Zoë didn't hesitate to gather four of the yellow fruit from the low branches of the nearest tree and carry them back to the platform. Jhezra bit into hers immediately and Alex followed suit but Zoë tasted hers before giving one to Laura.

'It tastes like mango juice,' she said. 'But it's juicy like oranges although the peel is very thin. I think you can eat all of it.' She put the round yellow fruit carefully into Laura's outstretched hand and savoured the rest of her own as the others ate.

'You're right,' Alex said to Jhezra when he'd finished eating. 'This place does look as if it's been planned for world-travellers.' He glanced at the cup standing again on the side of the basin. 'But they don't seem to be very technically advanced.'

'They build in stone,' Jhezra said tonelessly. 'That is not easy to do.'

'They make things out of clay,' Zoë added, trying to break the tension. 'And fire and glaze them.' She picked up the cup and studied it more carefully. 'There's no maker's mark though.'

'Or anything else to show the name of this place,' Alex agreed, looking around the platform.

'What now then?' Jhezra asked, unexpectedly turning to Zoë. 'Do we continue through the Library or explore this place so we can thank its people for their kindness?'

Put that way, Zoë thought they had better go on but she was surprised when Alex replied suddenly.

'I don't see much point in staying. After all, we can

always come back here. And Zoë's right that the world here might be dangerous. We should go back into the Library and look at the books nearby to see if there's something about this place.'

Not sure what to think of that Zoë looked over at Laura and found her re-tying the scarf in place over her eyes.

'I'm still blind,' she said. 'Perhaps these people could cure me, and help any of the rest of you who are hurt.'

No one said anything for a moment and Zoë realized they were waiting for her to speak.

'Oh, let's look around,' she agreed, uncomfortably. 'Jhẹzra's right that this seems like a good place.' Stepping back onto the platform she touched Laura's arm. 'There's a step,' she said. 'Shall I guide you?'

Morgan and her companions had left the inn early in the morning and set off on the road again. Ciren and Charm were in a hurry to move on and Kal had accepted their leadership of the group without argument. Despite the comfort of their rooms, after three days of camping across the mountains she hadn't slept well.

The twins had been noncommittal when she confessed to having told Kal about the existence of the Collegiate and she suspected it hadn't come as much of a surprise. Kal in turn had stayed silent when the twins had said they intended to take the nearest Door back into the Great Library and that they thought it would be best if Morgan and Kal came with them.

'If I'm going to be a world-traveller I think I should probably find out more about it,' she'd explained and Kal had nodded.

'I'd like to know more about it myself,' he'd agreed.

The twins hadn't replied to that although they appeared to have accepted Kal's presence in the group.

But increasingly Morgan was becoming conscious of how little she knew them or what they were capable of. Back in Shattershard they'd appeared like guardian angels out of a maelstrom of falling masonry and gunpowder smoke to rescue her. Now she wondered how they'd managed it.

Riding along side by side down the road in the bright early morning sunshine Ciren and Charm looked like a force to be reckoned with. Still dressed completely in magician's black, they looked less like teenagers of her own age than stunted aliens of another race. The similarity in their pale pointed faces and their dead straight white-blond hair and their slanted violet eyes wasn't the likeness of siblings. It was the eerie artificiality of design; like painted figures on a deck of divination cards: Twins.

More than that, Morgan was beginning to feel a bit alarmed by exactly how efficient Ciren and Charm were. Coming through the mountains they had passed other refugees on the road and had always seemed to come out of the encounter better than before. Ciren had bargained and bartered with everyone to pass by while Charm stayed silent at his side with a sweet smile on her lips. Having left Shattershard with two ponies, one light pack, and the clothes they had on their backs the party now had four ponies and a pack-horse loaded with gear, not to mention the weapons that the twins had worn openly since leaving the city: Charm's matched daggers and Ciren's long bow.

'How do you manage to be so prepared for everything?' Morgan asked, chivvying her pony up closer to Ciren as the more approachable of the twins. 'I can't believe the amount of baggage we've picked up.'

'It's a matter of circumstance,' Ciren said with a quick smile back at her. 'It's better to be prepared for as many eventualities as possible so we tend to travel with a wide assortment of kit. But in an emergency we pare down to essentials.'

'Essentials being?' Kal asked curiously and Charm joined in the conversation suddenly.

'Most are what any traveller would take,' she said. 'Something to spark a fire, travel rations, water, and a weapon.'

'Needle and thread,' Ciren said and lifted his eyebrows at Morgan's look of surprise. 'Easy to carry and can be used for sewing up wounds as well as clothes.'

Morgan winced at that but Kal was nodding thoughtfully.

'Medicines tend to be heavy but I imagine you've brought at least some of them. Unless either of you is a healer . . . ?'

Ciren gave Kal a searching look for a second before replying.

'Neither of us has healing magic,' he said slowly. 'But there are certain forms of damage I can heal. There are certain basic principles to medicine which apply everywhere although you'd be surprised at the variety of treatments.'

'I hadn't thought of that,' Morgan said, her mind flashing back to Earth and to hospitals and burn wards and radiotherapy and penicillin. 'I'm used to the way my own world deals with illness. I don't know anything about medicine here.' She shook her head in amazement. 'I'm just starting to realize how much there is to know.'

For a few minutes there was silence except for the clopping of the ponies' hooves down the track and tinkling birdsong somewhere in the distance. Then Ciren looked over at Morgan seriously.

'That's why you need to come to the Great Library,' he said. 'Not only does it have the answers to your questions, it asks others you haven't even thought to ask yet.'

'My father once told me that no question has just one answer,' Kal said abruptly. 'And not all answers are accurate.' It was Charm that he spoke to as the others looked at him awkwardly. 'What kind of answer will the Library have for me?'

The stand of fruit trees opened up at the other end of the clearing into an avenue. Zoë led Laura along the grassy pathway carefully while Jhezra led the way and Alex hung back more cautiously. Not more than about twenty paces down the avenue the fruit trees came to an end and they found themselves standing at the edge of a flowered meadow where the path cut a swath through the tall grass. A little distance away Zoë could clearly see a cluster of buildings on a low rise in the land.

As they walked through the meadow Zoë described it to Laura but was brought up short in the middle of describing the brilliant blue and purple colours of the wild-flowers.

'All right, Zoë, it's a field,' Laura said, cutting her off. 'What about the village?'

'It's too far away to make out any details,' Zoë told her and continued on in silence until Jhezra up ahead halted at the meadow's edge.

'There's a stream here,' she called back to them and as the others joined her she indicated a small creek that flowed along the side of the meadow and a little wooden bridge connecting the path to the opposite bank.

The bridge was made of wood, mounted on long timbers driven into the stream bed with firmly secured planks and a smoothed handrail on either side. It looked perfectly safe and Zoë didn't hesitate to lead Laura across it but halfway over the bridge she paused, seeing the village properly for the first time: a set of little wooden houses with chimneys puffing out thin white smoke.

'They are farmers,' Jhezra said, pointing out the fields

that could be seen further downstream. 'And . . . ' she turned to look upstream and squinted into the sun. 'I see animals of some kind on that hillside.'

'You have better eyesight than me,' Zoë said, looking where Jhezra was pointing. 'I see sort of brown blobs.'

'Me too,' Alex agreed, looking away. 'I can't see any people in the village either.'

'Well, I certainly can't see anything,' Laura said sharply, still standing where Zoë had left her in the centre of the bridge. 'Can we go on now?'

'Oh, sorry,' Zoë said, coming quickly to join Laura and taking her arm again. 'At the end of the bridge the path starts again but someone's laid pebbles on it so it might be a bit bumpy. Be careful as you walk.'

Laura didn't answer her but she placed her feet cautiously on the path as they came over the bridge.

The village was made up of no more than ten or twelve individual houses and lay spread out in a y-shape on the hillside ahead. The wide cobbled street ran up the hill for a short distance before dividing around a raised stone well. Jhezra had taken the lead as they crossed the bridge and as she walked up the street she turned and raised her hand suddenly, indicating a flash of movement ahead.

There was a little girl dressed in a brown smock crossing the cobbled triangle ahead. She was holding a wooden bucket and Zoë watched the child place the bucket carefully by the side of the well and reach up to wind the windlass on the side. It was such a commonplace domestic scene that Zoë felt reluctant to disturb her but by the time she'd caught up with Jhezra the child had filled her bucket with water and was carrying it carefully over to the side of the square and into the wide open entrance of a large wooden building.

'I think this is a shop of some kind,' Jhezra said as Zoë joined her.

'It's a forge,' said Alex unexpectedly behind them. 'Look at that steam.'

Zoë looked up and saw the puffs of white rising from one of two stone chimneys built into the side wall of the house and looked back again to see that Alex was walking forward.

'Well, shall we go in?' Laura asked a bit sarcastically and Zoë realized she was waiting to be guided. Jhezra had fallen in beside Alex and as the four of them walked up to the building Zoë heard a dull clank of metal on metal from somewhere inside.

The wooden house had two large doors a bit like a stable's which were thrown open but inside it was darker than Zoë had expected and she had to blink to adjust her eyes. As she hesitated Laura stepped forward and she had to follow quickly so as not to lose her balance. The heat of the forge glowed red at the back of the room and as they entered a large figure turned from the fire's heat to regard them with a steady gaze.

'Sun shine on you,' he said. 'And what may I do for you?'

There was a small sound from the side of the room and Zoë glanced over to see the little girl who had carried water staring at them wide-eyed from her seat at a long trestle table.

'Good morning,' Zoë said automatically and Laura at her side turned her face in the direction of the stranger.

'We're travellers, and I'm hoping you can help us . . . ' Alex began to say to the blacksmith but Zoë was still watching the little girl. Her hair was dark brown and in two neat plaits and her eyes were brown too and wide as she stared at them, looking as if she wasn't sure whether to run away. A movement at her side made her glance at Jhezra and she saw she was looking at the child too.

'Don't be afraid,' Jhezra said, smiling reassuringly.

'We're thankful for your people's kindness in leaving water and fruit for us.'

Alex paused in his introduction and Zoë saw that the blacksmith had turned to watch Jhezra and Zoë was uncomfortably conscious of the Hajhi girl's weapons.

'I'm sorry,' the little girl said uncertainly, still looking at Jhezra. 'I don't understand what you said.' She glanced at the blacksmith for support before turning suddenly to Zoë with a look of appeal.

'I'm sorry you didn't understand my friend,' Zoë said carefully. 'She said it was kind of your people to leave water by the Door and fruit in the orchard because we thought they were left for us.'

'Oh!' A beam of understanding spread across the child's face and she turned to smile back at Jhezra. But before she could say anything else the blacksmith drew their eyes to him again as he crossed to stand beside the child.

'You came from the Door,' he said and it was a statement rather than a question. 'You are welcome to the hospitality of our village. Unfortunately my daughter Averly,' he looked down at the little girl, 'is right when she says that your companion's speech lacks meaning for us.'

Zoë glanced at Jhezra in confusion but Alex was looking annoyed, as if he'd suddenly realized something, and Laura stepped smoothly into the breach.

'Jhezra doesn't have translation magic,' she said and Zoë remembered the amulet Laura had bought her in Shattershard with a sudden surprise. Laura and Alex wore them too but she'd never seen Jhezra wearing one. 'If you know about the Door in the orchard then you must know about world-travellers. We have been travelling for some days without food and water and are in need of your help.'

'Certainly.' The blacksmith's face switched abruptly from serious to concerned and he turned to the little girl but she was already moving towards a side door of the house.

'I'll call Katryn, shall I?' she said, looking to her father for approval.

'And then run to the herber's and fetch Taryn,' he agreed, already ushering them to seats at the trestle table. 'My name is Dynan, and I bid you be welcome in my house.'

Heading towards the heart of the Tetrarchate and with the ruins of his former life buried beneath the mountains Kal felt disconnected from his own world. He had lived all his life in Shattershard on the borders of the Tetrarchate Empire and surrounded by the dangers of the desert and the tempestuous Hajhim. He'd always assumed his life would end there as well once he had succeeded his father as ruler of the fortress city. But now he rode in the company of mages from different worlds and the only sign of his history was in the silver mesh of the Archon's crown.

Everything was strange to him here. The wooded hills that they rode through and twittering birdsong and rustlings of small animals in the bushes were already a world away from the shifting sands and barren rock of his home. Even the sun was different, shedding a lazy warmth across the morning instead of the merciless glare which beat down upon the desert.

'Is your world like this?' he asked suddenly, bringing Morgan out of a daydream of her own to look at him. 'So green and full of life?'

'I suppose so,' she said, shrugging, then she shook her head. 'No, maybe not. Where I lived, in England, was a bit like this, although the trees weren't so colourful. But a world isn't all the same all over, you know. We had mountains and deserts on Earth too.'

'And what about you?' Kal asked, seeing Ciren watching them. 'What's your world like?'

'We don't have one,' Charm said, letting her pony fall back alongside them. 'We were brought up in the Great Library.'

'It's our world for all intents and purposes,' Ciren agreed and Morgan looked fascinated.

'So is it a world?' she asked. 'A planet, I mean . . . ' She looked across at Kal for a moment, checking that he understood. 'Earth is a sphere, floating in space. Isn't this world the same?'

'A sphere?' he asked, feeling suddenly confused but Charm was already answering.

'The Great Library goes on forever,' she said.

'No one knows how far it extends,' Ciren added.

Still wondering what Morgan had meant by her world being a sphere Kal dropped the subject but a little later he realized that for once the twins hadn't said exactly the same thing.

He didn't mention it again but he stored the fact away for future consideration. If even Ciren and Charm who had grown up in the Great Library knew so little about it, what kind of place was it after all? Watching the road ahead beginning to climb down out of the foothills Kal found himself becoming impatient to take his first step through a Door.

Laura sat at the trestle table trying to sort the flurry of noises that surrounded her out in her head. It was curious to be starting out again in a new world and handicapped by her state as a blind person. The strip of material that covered her eyes was uncomfortably tight around her head.

Zoë had suggested that the spell Morgan cast might have been something like a flash glare and that resting her eyes would help. But Laura had checked each time they paused and the blackness she saw was absolute.

She'd had a lot of time to think as they walked through the empty corridors of the Great Library. Back on Earth she'd never suspected that the Door Between Worlds might be one of hundreds, or even thousands or millions. She'd found the Door in the Weywode Forest with Morgan and Alex and by keeping it to themselves they'd almost pretended that it wasn't real. Besides, in Shattershard they'd been treated like adults and Laura had been able to take full advantage of that. Here they were being treated like children.

Dynan the blacksmith had urged them to take seats at the trestle table and had been joined shortly by his wife, Katryn, while the child Averly had gone pattering out of the door on her bare feet to fetch some kind of healer. Zoë had helped Laura on to the bench attached to the table before launching into an explanation of who they were and how they had come here in between effusive expressions of thanks.

'We'd been travelling for three days when we found this place,' she was saying now somewhere across the room. 'And before that we were in an earthquake and a battlefield.'

'My heart goes out to you!' Katryn's voice was a warm contralto, lifting and falling as she crossed the room back and forth. 'Three days wandering? What can I get you? I was about to make soup but you won't want to wait for that. Let me give you some water at least.'

'We came through the Door on the other side of the river,' Zoë continued, still eager to explain herself. 'And we had a little water from the basin there and we took some fruit. I hope that's all right?'

'Bless you, that's what it's there for,' the village woman said warmly. 'But have a little more to drink now and when the herber's seen to you I'll fetch you out some bread and greens.'

Laura started when she heard a sudden splashing of water close by and felt a cup being pushed firmly into her hands.

'There you go, child,' Katryn said, before addressing Zoë over Laura's head. 'Sit down, bless you, you must be tired too leading your friend all this way. Has she hurt her eyes?'

'She was blinded in a magical accident,' Alex announced in lordly tones. 'And I was wounded in the battle my companion mentioned. The rest is just bruises and grazes but we'd be glad if the herber—you said her name was Taryn?—we'd be grateful if she can help us.'

'Of course,' Katryn assured him. 'But do you rest easy now while we wait for the herber.'

'My name is Laura,' Laura said, lifting her head and addressing the space from which Katryn had last spoken. 'Thank you for the water.'

'You're very kind,' Jhezra added and Laura tried to conceal her impatience as they went through another rigmarole of Zoë translating. Really Alex should have got Jhezra a translation amulet months ago instead of just relying on his to translate for them, this was getting ridiculous.

'It's a spell,' Zoë was beginning to explain but she was cut off by the sound of a new arrival.

It was obviously Averly returned with the herb-woman and Laura decided that it would probably be a good idea to stay here for a while. After all that useless wandering in the Library here were people ready and willing to give them everything they needed. She hoped Zoë would have the sense not to bring up the question of payment.

'I'm here,' a sharp female voice said suddenly. 'Who's the most in need of treatment?'

'Alex, I think,' said Zoë and Laura had to wait as Taryn unpacked what sounded like a whole pharmacopoeia of medicines onto the table, some of which smelt strongly like camphor.

'I'll need fresh bandages, Katryn,' the herb-woman was saying. 'And boiled water as well. And, Averly, you run back to my linen closet and get a couple of clean shirts, hurry now.'

'Can Jhezra or I help?' Zoë asked as Averly went scampering off again in another patter of bare feet.

Katryn was clanking pots and pans about in the next room and between Zoë's efforts to help the herb-woman, and Alex's curses when she removed the makeshift bandages and Jhezra's inability to make herself understood there was an endless stream of conversation across Laura's head. For a moment she thought back to her residence in Shattershard and the quiet deference of her Hajhi servants and with an extra pang of regret for the power and influence she'd built up there. Taking a sip from her cup of water she wondered how she could take control over her life again.

It wasn't until the travellers stopped for the night that Charm and Ciren had the opportunity to speak in private. They came off the road at dusk and went a little way into the woods to make their camp in a small clearing among the red-leaved trees.

Back at the inn Ciren had bargained for two tents, neither as good as the one the twins had left in Shattershard, but good enough for the gentler climate of the Tetrarchate homelands. While Morgan and Kal set theirs up on one side of the clearing Charm swiftly assembled the other on the opposite side while Ciren attended to the ponies. By the time Morgan and Kal were finished the twins had already built a small cooking fire and for a while they talked together around its cheerful warmth. But once they'd finished eating the fire died down and they'd retreated to the shelter of their tents.

As she updated their book with an account of the day's journey, Charm could hear the murmur of voices from across the clearing but no individual words. Still, when Ciren returned from stowing the cooking gear, she spoke softly.

'Kal is suspicious,' she said.

'It's only natural,' Ciren said quickly and Charm put aside the book to look at him properly. As always he seemed edgy on the subject of the boy Archon and she wanted to understand why.

'His questions are searching,' she said slowly, biting her lips. 'He asks about our magic, about the Library, about our home world . . . '

'Why shouldn't he ask?' Ciren said, not meeting her eyes as he laid out their bedrolls neatly side by side. 'Morgan had the same questions when we first initiated her.'

'Morgan will be one of us.'

'And so will Kal be.' Ciren's voice was patient but there was a tenseness about him that Charm found uncomfortable.

'Morgan accepted our answers,' she said, wondering why her twin seemed so slow to reach her conclusions. 'How long do you think Kal will?'

Ciren raised his head then and looked at her searchingly and Charm frowned under his study. It was the same disjunction between them she had noticed the night before; the same questioning gaze he'd been watching her with ever since they'd started travelling with Kal and Morgan.

'I wish you'd tell me what you're thinking now,' she said, meeting his eyes.

'I wish it was something I could put into words,' Ciren replied instantly with a flash of their old affinity.

'I could . . . ' Charm began but Ciren was already shaking his head.

'Don't smile,' he said quickly. 'I don't want you to read me.'

'I don't,' she said at once, stiffening with tension. 'I never have.' Her mouth twisted in a grimace as she tried to keep control of her expression and she wondered what Ciren was suddenly thinking that he felt the need to ask for something that had never been an issue between them before.

'You've never had a reason to before,' he said, answering her eventually and Charm looked away.

'You've never had a thought you couldn't say before either,' she said, her voice still low. 'But I don't have to read you to know that you don't trust me. What you have said is evidence enough of that.'

Charm waited for her twin's response but minutes passed in silence and she realized that he didn't have anything to say to her. Instead she finished her last comments in the book and put the light out. As she lay down on her bedroll she realized that the voices of the others had fallen silent as well and the only sound left was Ciren's even breathing in the close darkness of the tent. Closing her eyes, Charm found herself matching her breathing to his as she waited to fall asleep.

3

At the top of the hill above the Village the wind buffeted Laura's face, whipping up her hair and tossing it into a tangled mess. Frowning to herself she smoothed it back, her fingers twisting it into a long plait that held it back even without a tie or ribbon.

Laura knew what she would see if she wasn't blind. Zoë had described the view to her on the first day and as far as she could tell nothing had changed. Further down the hill the buildings of the Village nestled together; the herber's hut was the furthest away here on the crest of the hill. Then came the snaking line of the river and beyond that the trees that cloaked the Door into the Library. Villagers and their animals would be dotted around that landscape, everyone immersed in some worthy activity.

Over the past few days Alex had pestered the herber with questions about this world, asking about cities and trade roads, kings and governments, weapons and magic. Laura could have told him it wouldn't be of any use. These people were hopeless provincials. None of them had any interest in anything beyond the next valley, let alone in other worlds. Perhaps with the right motivation something might spur them into action but Laura doubted it. Generations would be born and die here, living exactly the same way their ancestors had before them.

Alex's questions had finally died down and Laura knew he was impatient to leave this place. Maybe to Zoë or Jhezra, who hadn't properly experienced life in another world before, this was impressive. But in Shattershard the Harrells had lived the life of powerful aristocrats and Alex wanted that back. Unfortunately for him all his plans had been based on taking over Shattershard and ruling it with the help of the Hajhim. Luckily for Laura she could see further even though she was blind.

Beyond the Village lay the Library and Doors into hundreds of worlds. Worlds which like Shattershard had rulers and armies, cities and kingdoms and guilds. Laura had learnt in Shattershard that any system could be manipulated provided that you knew the rules. While Alex had charged about with a sword, becoming part of the Hajhi war-band and trading on his scientific knowledge, Laura's skill was with people, manipulating them for her own ends.

Losing everything they had worked for in Shattershard was an annoyance, being cut off from their route back to Earth an irrelevance: Laura had never had any intention of going home anyway. From the moment they'd discovered their first Door she'd known what she wanted: a world of her own. Now she was as far away from that ambition as ever but she had no intention of giving it up.

The wind continued to bluster past, the cold breeze blocking out the warmth of the sun she couldn't see. But Laura continued to stand on the top of the hill staring out across her imagined view of the world, towards an infinity of possibilities, planning the path she would have to take towards her goal.

During their journey to the capital city of the Tetrarchate Morgan realized how much her opinion of the world had been shaped by her time in Shattershard. On the other side of the mountains the land was a series of forested hills and cultivated valleys. Although Ciren and Charm had chosen a route that skirted along the hillside roads Morgan occasionally caught a glimpse of a walled city filling a valley or snaking along the banks of a river. Like Shattershard they had high towers and bridges although none of them were as grimly impressive as the black heights of the desert fortress.

The only people they passed on the lonely hillside roads were peasants who scurried to get out of the way of the horses. The twins rode ahead always and although Ciren occasionally glanced down at the people they passed Charm only noticed if they came close when she focused her purple-black eyes upon them and watched them with a curious smile as they passed by.

'What is the Tetrarchate then?' Morgan asked curiously, as she watched another distant vista of city towers vanish behind them. 'How does it work?'

'It's the ruling government of most of our world,' Kal told her, and Morgan sensed that Ciren and Charm had reined their horses in so that they could listen to what he said. 'Shattershard and the desert were on the borderland of their influence but all of the territories we've passed are under Tetrarchate control.'

'Laura and Alex thought otherwise,' Morgan began carefully. 'They claimed Shattershard was under the thumb of the Tetrarchate.'

Kal shot her a cool grey glance and then looked down at his pony, steadying it.

'It was difficult,' he said eventually. 'Historically Shattershard was a fortress but when I was young it had been a trade city for several generations. We dealt with the Tetrarchate on one side and the Hajhim on the other. But since my father died it's been . . . it was . . . harder to quarrel with the interests of the Tetrarchate. It was they who decided the Hajhim had become a problem and sent troops to crush them.'

A bird floated on a thermal breeze high in the air and Morgan wondered what it was like for Kal to have governed a city. Compared to him she felt young and inexperienced.

'It's unfortunate,' Ciren said so softly that it took Morgan a moment to realize he was speaking at all, 'that the Tetrarchate troops sparked off so violent a conflict.'

'But would such a conflict have arisen if not for those uninitiated world-travellers selling arms to the Hajhim?' Charm said suddenly. 'The Tetrarchate troops were sent to bring peace to the area.'

'Peace?' Kal shot her a swift glance. 'The Tetrarchate have brought many cities under their peace. This is my world and I have heard its history for all of my life. The Tetrarchate was once one city, Shimmering on the horizon, and like Shattershard all the other cities had their own Archons and Barons and Guild Masters. But the Archon of Shimmering brought other cities beneath his own rule and the guilds and the politicians worked with him so that now the Tetrarchate rules across all the fertile lands of our world and only in the deserts and swamps can the borderland cities remain free of their influence.'

The twins had said nothing to that but Morgan had wondered what they thought of the world of the Tetrarchate. They'd told her in Shattershard that they'd visited hundreds of worlds and now she wondered how they'd see one world compared to so many more.

As they finally approached the capital city of the Tetrarchate Morgan thought they'd reached the sea. The blue-white glitter on the horizon seemed to shimmer like the crests of waves breaking on a shore. But as the road headed unerringly closer, climbing down from the hills towards the city, she'd begun to make out the shapes of walls and towers in the glimmering sparkles of light.

'What makes it shine like that?' she asked and Ciren replied in a matter-of-fact way.

'The stone it's built with has iridescent properties,' he said.

'The blue coloration is typical of the rock of the region,' Charm added without any especial sign of interest.

Kal said nothing but as they made their way into the increasingly tangled streets of the city his eyes drifted to note their surroundings. It was late and Morgan's impression of the outskirts of the city was a haze of dim flashes in the evening light. A troop of city guards on horseback, a coffee-house with patrons seated around tables in an outside garden, a crew of road workers repairing a broken pavement. When the twins booked two rooms in a blockish hostelry it was a relief to be out of the strange blue-grey night and, as Ciren and Charm took the ponies to be stabled, Morgan watched them leave from the window of her room.

'They are always so distant,' Kal said suddenly from behind her. 'If I become a world-traveller I wonder how it will change me.'

'I've already left my world behind,' Morgan said, still looking out into the twilight. 'And who I am seems to change all the time.'

* * *

Sitting at the long wooden table in the forge's kitchen Zoë methodically sliced sections of bitter-root for the midday meal. She'd found it relaxing to settle into the simple life of the Village, so different from the complicated politics of Shattershard. But as peaceful as it was here, it still wasn't home.

Dynan the blacksmith had offered them a room in his home while their injuries healed but the herber had taken Alex and Laura away to her own house. The Village seemed to operate as a large extended family. Taryn the herber had turned out to be Dynan's mother and the other people they met were also all related in one sense or another. Katryn, Dynan's wife, seemed to do a lot of the cooking for the rest of the Village, as well as baking bread, preparing dyes, and weaving cloth. But everyone here seemed to have several professions at once and even Averly, the blacksmith's little girl, was kept constantly on the hop running errands back and forth through the Village.

In the middle of such a hive of industry Zoë would have felt awkward not helping out. Although the Village had been soothing after their three long days lost in the Library she still felt out of place. After the drama surrounding Shattershard the quiet life of the village was a striking contrast and arriving here as battle-scarred strangers had made Zoë feel odd. She'd hung up the cream leather army coat her dad had given her on the back of the door of her room and borrowed Katryn's shawl if she had to go out in the evening. But however much she tried to join in she could feel the difference between her and the rest of the Villagers. Perhaps it was because they never asked questions about where the strangers had come from, taking their presence for granted as they discussed the details of their own affairs instead.

Finishing with the bitter-root, Zoë added the slices to

the casserole simmering gently in Katryn's clay oven and then wiped the table down for the fourth time that day. Katryn was fastidious about keeping her kitchen clean and given that the same table was used to prepare dyes, dry herbs, and make up medicines as well as preparing food, Zoë could understand why.

'Zoë? Are you busy?' Jhezra came in as she finished wiping down the table and perched on the bench at the side.

'Not right now.' Zoë checked her watch automatically. 'But I need to gather some fruit for dinner soon.'

'May I come with you?' Jhezra asked with her customary politeness. 'There's something I would speak with you about and we could talk on the way.'

'Of course,' Zoë told her, getting the large basket from its peg on the wall. Before she left she glanced once more around the room to check everything was as it should be and then followed Jhezra out into the lazy afternoon sunshine.

Jhezra seemed to have fitted into Village life even better than Zoë had, she reflected as they set off down the cobbled street. At first Zoë had worried about her, the only one of their group without a translation amulet, but as it turned out Jhezra hadn't had a problem. Without the automatic translation provided by the amulet Jhezra had picked up several words of the Villagers' language on the first day and had been adding to her vocabulary ever since. She'd spent most of her time with Averly, helping the little girl fetch and carry, and Zoë often heard them chattering together as they went in and out of the house.

'You seem almost fluent in the language here by now,' she said out loud as they came out of the village and crossed the bridge over the stream.

'Not nearly,' Jhezra said, laughing as she shook her head. 'It seemed a good plan to try to learn the local speech.' She paused for a second and then added: 'But it won't be much use anywhere else.'

'It's a pity we couldn't get another translation amulet for you,' Zoë admitted. 'But the people here don't seem to use magic at all.'

'I'm not so certain,' Jhezra said seriously. 'I don't know much about spells but Taryn is a skilled enough healer that perhaps there is magic in her herb-craft.'

'But not enough to cure Laura.'

'You shouldn't despair,' Jhezra said, obviously trying to be consoling. 'Perhaps a healer with greater skill may be able to help her.'

'I think it'll take a magician,' Zoë said honestly. 'Morgan cast the spell on her in the first place. I think we'll have to find another magician who can take it off again.'

'If we are to do that we will have to leave here,' Jhezra said and Zoë glanced across at her.

They'd reached the fruit trees by now and, without consulting with each other, they walked down the avenue towards the central clearing together. There was the stone platform and the black oval of the Door Between Worlds, not looking as out of place as it might enclosed in the sunny ring of fruit trees. Putting down the basket, they began to gather golden-fruit.

'So what do you plan to do next?' Jhezra asked as they worked. 'Alexander is well now and Laura not likely to get any better . . . '

'I suppose we should go into the Library again,' Zoë said uncertainly. 'Perhaps we can find a way back to our own worlds. But I'm not sure how to begin.'

'If we go back through the Door we could be wandering for ages before we found any people or a place as friendly as this,' Jhezra pointed out.

'They are friendly,' Zoë agreed. 'But . . . ' she turned

to look at the empty black space of the Door, 'it's not home.'

Ever since seeing the number of Doors they'd passed in the Library Zoë realized that it wouldn't be an easy task to find a way back to Earth among what might be millions of possible worlds. She wondered if it would be more sensible to stay in this safe and peaceful place instead of risking unknown dangers. But she couldn't help it. Even if going home was a hopeless quest she had to try.

She looked seriously at Jhezra. 'I'm not like Laura and Alex,' she said. 'Or even Morgan. I didn't have a secret life on another world. I wasn't intending to have adventures or be in battles, I just wanted to see what it was like.' She sighed. 'And now I'm a million miles away from Earth and I just want to get back.'

'I'm sorry,' Jhezra said and Zoë felt guilty. She hadn't meant to blame the other girl for what had happened but Jhezra could easily have taken her words that way.

'It's not your fault . . . ' she began but Jhezra chopped her words off with a sharp gesture.

'What happened in the past is done now,' she said. 'But we have decisions ahead of us. If you want to find your world, I will help you.'

When they'd left Morgan and Kal at the rooming house the twins had more business than tending to the ponies. That had taken only a few minutes, since there was a public stable only a few blocks away, but they had more than one reason for wanting to be alone.

By the time they left the stable the sun was setting over the city but pale rose strings of lamps lit up along the highways and byways and set the buildings glittering wildly in their borrowed light. More people were out on the streets now that the wine-shops and coffee-houses had opened. But in their magician's blacks the twins were given ample space as they made their way through the crowds.

Their destination was a building in the temple district, a round bluestone structure with a scintillating dome that was visible from streets away. At the entrance an offertory bowl was prominently displayed with a red-robed priest standing beside it in case any of the faithful should feel tempted by the pile of coins it contained. The priest coughed slightly as the twins approached and Ciren dropped a few coins into the bowl at his prompting.

'A waste of money,' Charm said softly as they entered the temple and Ciren flicked his eyes at her.

'We'll be leaving soon anyway,' he said. 'Besides, this currency's no use to us anywhere else.'

Huge candelabras stood here and there across the temple floor and the twins made their way past them towards the inner sanctum. Another priest guarded the door here and this time Ciren stopped to speak to him.

'We have business with the Second Elder,' he said briefly. 'Will you tell him that Ciren and Charm are here?'

'With great pleasure,' the priest replied with a bow but he didn't move until Ciren produced another few coins for him.

As they waited by the door the twins stood in silence. Although they hadn't spoken of the subject since their first night in the woods the shadow of that conversation still hung over them like a palpable force. In the past they'd always shared comfortable silences together but now they both watched the door, uneasy with even a minor delay, feeling the pressure of things unsaid. It was a relief when the priest returned.

'The Second will see you now,' he said, opening the door for them and this time Ciren didn't give him money for the service.

The lights in the inner sanctum were brighter still and priests hurried hither and thither preparing for the next service with piles of glowingly embroidered robes and censers streaming with pungent incense, their garments tinkling with charms and bells. Ciren and Charm threaded their way through the preparations to a side chapel where a large round figure stood waiting for them, swathed in the voluminous folds of a rich velvet robe.

'Well met, noble lords,' the Second Elder said as they entered, making a swift pass across his chest to flip out a round red and black symbol worn on a chain about his neck. He was as bald as an egg and his fat florid face almost as red as his clothes and he smiled widely at the twins as he hid the symbol again under his priest's robes. 'It's honour enough to receive you.'

'And greetings to you,' Ciren said politely while at his side Charm allowed herself a small polite smile.

'May I offer you refreshments?' the Second Elder asked. 'Wine, perhaps? Or we have a fine selection of brandies if that's more to your taste.'

'Thank you, no,' Ciren told him. 'We are short on time tonight. We came only to inform you of our return to this city and of our imminent plans to return through the Door tomorrow. How fares our embassy here?'

'Oh, very well indeed.' The bald man's fat smile grew wider still at the question. 'The Door has been secured and our agents are ensconced in several positions of influence throughout the city.' He glanced down at his own red robe momentarily and smoothed the golden embroidered sleeves into place. 'Naturally we've been sending regular reports back to our superiors in the Wheel but if you speak to them in person I hope you can report how smooth our success has been here. The Tetrarchate should be fully under our influence within a year.'

As the Second Elder spoke Charm's small smile

remained on her lips and she watched the thoughts shuffling rapidly through his head. He was a Wheel agent of some years' standing, his own home-world one with a similarly corrupted government to the Tetrarchate, and he seemed to be thriving as a temple priest. He was one of the type of agent who enjoyed the trappings of wealth and position on the worlds he was sent to infiltrate but didn't have much power or influence within the Wheel itself. Although he was painting a rosier picture than was strictly accurate, from what he was thinking it was clear that the Wheel's embassy here had indeed been successful. In fact the extreme friendliness of the Second Elder seemed quite genuine and his thoughts were mostly on how best to ingratiate himself with them.

Losing interest, Charm pulled back out of his mind and waited for Ciren to conclude their business here.

' . . . sure I can't tempt you to a morsel of food?' the priest was saying. 'My acolytes can bring it in moments.'

'No, we must be going now,' Ciren said briskly. 'But if you would have someone send word to the embassy to expect us tomorrow morning, that would be appreciated.'

'Certainly, certainly, I'll have someone sent at once,' the Second Elder replied, hurrying over his farewells in his anxiousness to fulfil the request. 'I'll just show you the way out through the sanctuary first,' he continued, leading them towards a side door. 'The service is about to start in the main temple and you won't want to be mixed up in all that.'

'Thank you,' Ciren said again as they turned to leave. 'We appreciate your help.'

'No need for thanks, happy to be of service,' the priest insisted. 'Tell me,' he paused as he was opening the door, 'have you heard yet that those barbarians in the desert were crushed at last? Good news for the Wheel, there . . . if it's true, that is.'

'We've heard,' Ciren replied quellingly. 'It's true enough.'

'Well and good then,' the priest said smiling. 'Please do send my respects to your superiors. Always a pleasure to work with them.'

Walking up the hill to the herber's house that afternoon, Zoë was conscious of how long it had been since she'd really talked to Laura or Alex and she felt nervous about broaching the topic of leaving. To take her mind off it she concentrated on how warm the sunshine felt on her bare arms and how clear the air was so that she could see the gently rolling countryside in all directions. She could feel the pull of the climb in her legs as she walked up the hill and she wondered idly if she'd put on muscle as well as weight since the beginning of their stay here. Looking down at her arms she could tell that her skin was getting freckles of a tan although back on earth it would be nearly winter.

Taryn's house was smaller than Dynan's forge and was at the edge of the Village beside a small herb-garden where she grew her medicines. When Zoë arrived there was no sign of the herber but Alex was working in the garden, picking insects from the growing herbs, and he looked up with an expression of annoyance when she stopped next to him.

'Oh, it's you,' he said grumpily. 'What do you want?'

'I just wanted to talk for a bit,' Zoë said, trying to sound normal. 'Where's Laura?'

Alex shrugged and turned vaguely in the direction of the house before suddenly shouting:

'Laura!'

A shadow shifted by the entrance to the cottage and Laura moved out of the small porch, turning her blank face in their direction. She'd stopped wearing the bandage since Taryn's discovery that there was nothing physically wrong with her vision and Zoë found it difficult to look at her.

Laura's eyes were a clear green, a pale gooseberry colour that gave her a calm expression, but now she was blind there was something unnerving about the fixedness of her gaze as she stood unblinking in the sunlight. Zoë wondered uncomfortably how long Laura had just been standing there, waiting in silence, by the porch. But she smiled at the other girl and at Alex as she said:

'Can you stop work for a minute? I want to ask you something.'

'What's up?' Alex asked, leaving the plants and brushing the earth from his hands as he came to join her beside Laura. 'I could do with a break. The herb-woman's had me working like a slave out here all morning picking creepy crawlies off these bloody plants. What this place needs is a decent bug spray.'

Zoë ignored his complaint and leant against one of the stout wooden pillars of Taryn's porch as she spoke.

'I was talking to Jhezra earlier,' she said, 'and we were thinking that now that Alex is better maybe we should think about moving on.' She glanced over at Laura and met that blind gaze uncomfortably. 'Taryn hasn't been able to cure your blindness,' she added. 'We should maybe try and find a magical healer, don't you think?'

'Suits me,' Alex said, grimacing at the dirt on his hands. 'I'm ready to leave when you are. This place is all right as far as it goes but I've been thinking we should try and get back to some kind of civilization. I don't know about you but I don't want to spend the rest of my life as a gardening boy.'

'Or as a rustic peasant,' Laura agreed. Her mouth curled

a little as she added offhandedly: 'How've you been getting on with your lot?'

'Katryn's been very kind,' Zoë told her, feeling uncomfortable with the way Laura phrased her question.

'Lucky for us they're so generous,' Alex said casually. 'They don't seem to have any concept of money either.'

'Yeah, lucky for us,' Zoë echoed, before glancing over at Laura. 'How are you feeling?' she asked, touching her arm gently.

'I'm fine, Zoë,' Laura said. 'But do you really think my blindness is something that can be cured?'

'I hope so,' Zoë told her. But even as she said the words she wondered if they were at all true.

The twins brought back food with them when they returned to the rooming house and they ate together sitting in a circle on the floor of Morgan and Kal's room. Morgan found the spiced bread too hot to eat but Kal tore into it with gusto, sluicing it down with deep draughts of the thick black wine the twins had also brought back.

Ciren and Charm ate automatically as they had throughout the journey on a diet of travel stew and the rabbit-like creatures Ciren had snared in his traps. Neither of them ever seemed really interested in food although they had broken the journey for meals at the same point every day. Morgan wondered if they were even tasting what they ate but she was enjoying the first restaurant food she'd had since the last days before the destruction of Shattershard and finding out which combinations of meat and sauces worked well together. Back on Earth she'd been thinking about becoming a vegetarian but during her long days on the road she'd decided that world-travellers probably didn't have the luxury to be fastidious about what they ate.

She was halfway through her second glass of wine and deciding she couldn't eat even one more of the sweet pastries when one of the twins finally spoke.

'If the two of you are amenable we'll leave this world tomorrow,' Charm said. 'We made arrangements to sell the ponies and tack at the stable and I don't believe any of us have anything to keep us here any longer.'

It seemed callous to put it that way and Morgan looked anxiously over at Kal but he was refilling his glass again and only looked up at her movement.

'As you wish,' he said equitably. 'You realize I still know next to nothing about this Library of yours though.'

The twins looked at each other and then Ciren spoke quietly. He was fiddling with the stem of his untouched glass of wine and he didn't look at Kal as he spoke.

'Technically you are not a world-traveller until you have passed through your first Door,' he said, and his voice held a hint of weariness. 'And the Collegiate has a rule against telling our secrets to the uninitiated.'

'And does it have a rule about you stealing our secrets from us?' Kal asked, stretching his long legs out on the floor and looking over at Charm. 'You must know Morgan's told me you're a mind-reader.' He took another deep gulp of wine and Morgan realized he must be getting drunk.

The twins' expressions were always difficult to interpret but there was something like concern in Ciren's purple-black eyes which was mirrored and reflected back as anger in Charm's.

'I knew she was going to tell you before she knew it herself,' Charm said snappishly and glanced at Morgan with an air of triumph. 'Just because we didn't prevent it doesn't mean we weren't aware.'

'Because of course you're prepared for anything,' Kal

said laughingly towards Charm and her pointed face narrowed at him with annoyance.

'We helped you,' Ciren said gently to Morgan. 'And we'll tell you more once you're in the Library.' He looked at Kal as he added: 'You'll be one of us then.'

'If you obey the Collegiate's rules,' Charm added abruptly. She stood up, abandoning her full wine glass, and went to the doorway before turning to look down at Kal from across the room. 'Not everyone there is as understanding as us.' Her black-purple gaze shifted to Ciren and, seeming to read the expression in her eyes, her twin stood and went to join her.

'We'll leave you for now then,' he said. 'Be ready to leave tomorrow morning, please.' His look was at Morgan rather than Kal. 'I wouldn't stay up too late.'

They left, Ciren closing the door carefully behind him, and Morgan turned anxiously to her prince. He grinned at her and took another long sip of his wine and she frowned.

'I think you might have offended them,' she told him carefully.

'I had Charm going for a moment there, didn't I,' he replied, grinning at her over his wine glass and suddenly his words seemed less slurred. 'But Ciren I'm not so sure about. I think I worry him somehow.'

'What . . . what do you mean?' Morgan narrowed her eyes at him and Kal sipped his wine again before putting the glass down on the floor.

'It would take a bit more than that to make me drunk, my love,' he said smiling. 'Especially after all that spice-bread.' He reached out and slung an arm around her, pulling her alongside him as he added: 'Be careful how you kiss me, I'll set your mouth on fire.'

Morgan giggled and then squirmed to evade him when he dipped his head closer to her.

'All I can smell is your wine breath,' she said, glaring up at him. 'But why were you pretending to be drunk? Just to annoy them?'

'I've picked up a few tricks here and there,' Kal said, suddenly serious again. 'Your two friends are masters of doubletalk. They weave words like veils, as Jagannath would say. But thinking I was drunk they let a few things slip.'

'Let what slip?' Morgan goggled at him. 'They didn't tell you anything, did they?'

Kal's arm tightened a bit closer around her shoulders and he moved to smooth her hair with a gentle touch.

'Oh, they let something slip, my love,' he said. 'And it's not the first time. For all their talk of the fabulous organization of the Collegiate and the Great Library, when they first came to Shattershard they called themselves members of the order of the Wheel. They've never mentioned it again after that first introduction but both their cloaks have a symbol on the edge of the hood that's very like a red and black wheel.'

'That's true.' Morgan's mind raced as she thought back through her conversations with the twins and then she finally shook her head. 'So what do you think it means?'

'It means that we must be wary,' Kal said and his clear grey eyes met hers with open concern. 'And you most especially, my dearest love. Because I learnt something else tonight . . . Charm cannot read my mind.'

'She can't?' Morgan stared at him. 'But she can . . . it happens when she smiles. She said she knew I was going to tell you about the Collegiate before I knew it myself. And she found out about me being a world-traveller by seeing things about Earth in my mind when she met me.'

'And she must have tried to read my mind then and failed,' Kal said softly. 'I remember her smiling then. Look, Morgan, Charm was annoyed tonight. I baited her slightly and she's not exactly a subtle person. If she could have read my mind she'd have done it then and she'd have known that I wasn't as drunk as I pretended to be. She'd have pulled the same trick on me by saying something she knew from my mind to scare me with her power.' He smiled a bit grimly and added: 'She's not subtle but she's effective. Unfortunately she's blocked from reading me. And I think I can guess why.'

Morgan frowned and looked at him but he didn't speak and she had to work it out for herself.

'Your crown,' she said, reaching to touch the delicate silver meshwork wonderingly before shivering suddenly. 'You're lucky,' she said. 'I don't like her being able to read my mind.'

'No.' Kal put his arms around her and buried a kiss in her hair. 'I don't like that either.'

4

Morgan stepped through her second Door at midmorning Tetrarchate time. She'd washed and dressed early that morning and from the window of her room watched the streets of Shimmering gradually come alive with people. It could almost have been a city of Earth, she thought, as an endless parade of people walked back and forth beneath her window. If she'd come here in a different way, without Kal and the twins and the pressures of her history back in Shattershard, she would have liked to explore the city further. But already in her mind Morgan had moved on to wonder about the mysterious corridors of the Great Library.

Ciren and Charm had led the way out through the shining streets of the city in the direction of an area of new development to the east. A new street was being laid and the travellers had to skirt past the teams of road-workers heaving large blocks of glittering stone into place as they made their way through the building site.

'Where are we going?' Morgan asked, as the mass of

Shimmering fell behind and Ciren pointed out a building ahead halfway up a low hill outside the city.

'That's where the Door is,' he said. 'The house is owned by Collegiate members.'

'Behind those walls?' Kal asked and Charm turned to regard him levelly.

'It's important to protect the Door,' she told him. 'Remember this place. If you ever find yourself on this world again you should remember that this is a way through to the Library.' Then she turned to Morgan. 'And that this world is the only way you know back through your own Door to Earth.'

'I hadn't thought of that,' Morgan said, surprised at herself, and looked around her, trying to fix the place in her memory.

The newly-laid road ran out before they reached the house but in its place was a beaten track through the low furze of the hillside that led directly up to the front entrance set in the middle of a long high wall. At the gate Kal's eyes flickered towards Morgan and then across at a mosaic plaque set into one of the gateposts: a circular pattern of a red and black spoked wheel.

Ciren reached out to ring a heavy bell and moments later the gate opened to reveal a plainly dressed servant who looked at them expectantly.

'Ciren and Charm,' Ciren said. 'We are expected.'

'Your names are on my list,' the servant agreed, flipping open a leather-bound book. 'And the names of these others?'

'Kal khi Kalanthé,' Kal said, watching the servant as he took a pen from his pocket and inscribed something in swiftly flowing characters across a fresh page.

'Faction and Dignifiers?' the servant asked, glancing up at him expectantly, but Ciren spoke before Kal could say anything more.

'A Native, dignified as Archon of Shattershard,' he said and for a moment the servant seemed surprised before blanching at something in Ciren's expression and bowing a little to him as well as Kal before writing again in his book.

'And you, my lady?' the servant said, turning to Morgan next.

'My name is Morgan, I'm a member of the Guild of Magicians,' she said, remembering her apprenticeship in Shattershard. 'I don't know about faction,' she added before he could ask and looked across at the twins.

'Mark her as of the Wheel,' Charm said. 'She is our initiate,' she added to the servant.

'Thank you, Lord Archon, Lady Mage,' the servant said politely and stepped aside for them to pass through the gate.

On the other side of the gate everything had been carefully planned. The bulk of the house sat squarely in the middle of a neatly manicured garden which reminded Morgan of stately homes back in England. It was quiet on this side of the wall, away from the life of the thriving city, and the only sign of activity was a servant in the same plain livery as the gatekeeper who was carefully pruning a stand of thorny bushes.

To Morgan's surprise, Ciren and Charm didn't go up the path to the building but struck out along the side of the garden wall instead.

'The Door's not inside?' she asked.

'Buildings can collapse,' Charm said shortly, with a glance at Kal. 'It's wiser to leave them outside.'

Morgan hadn't even thought of the idea that Doors could be enclosed before and she found herself wondering if the one she and the twins had discovered in Shattershard beneath a great reservoir tank had been blocked off on purpose.

'So how long have you been using this Door, anyway?' she asked the twins and saw them exchange a look.

'Not long,' Ciren said carefully. 'We first came into this world only a few months ago. That was when the work on this structure was first put in hand.'

'You've managed to do a lot in such a short space of time,' Kal said neutrally but Ciren looked uncomfortable at the comment and didn't reply.

The garden went back some distance behind the house and the newly bedded plants gradually gave way to a wilder tangle of bracken and shrubbery which had been trimmed back enough to form a network of looping paths in and out of some russet-leaved trees. It was surprisingly like the Weywode Forest back on Earth but when they approached the Door the resemblance ended.

'Oh my God,' Morgan breathed softly as she saw what awaited them.

'Don't worry,' Ciren said with a look that was probably meant to be reassuring. 'They work for us.'

They were standing at the edge of a neat square of flagstones at the heart of the grove of trees. In the centre of the square the Door stood black and obvious in the morning sunlight but between it and them was a phalanx of guards. Half of them were wearing a kind of chain-mail that Morgan hadn't seen before on this world and carrying wicked-looking rapiers. But the other half were unarmed and the air of gentle menace they exuded came from the stark blackness of their magician's robes. Like Ciren and Charm their clothing was decorated with the same symbol of a black and red wheel.

'Are they from the Collegiate?' Morgan whispered to Ciren, feeling as if she was an obvious fraud in her own black clothes.

'Naturally,' he said, already walking towards the Door, and Morgan fell back and reached for Kal's hand.

'It looks like this is it,' she said nervously and he squeezed her hand briefly before letting it fall and taking hold of his sword hilt.

'Be ready for anything,' he murmured softly as Ciren and Charm approached the guards.

But to Morgan's surprise they weren't challenged. As the twins stepped forward the guards moved back a bit to give them a clear path towards the Door. Morgan and Kal followed after them and watched as first Ciren, then Charm, stepped through the hole in space without a backward glance. Kal raised his eyebrows at the sight and Morgan remembered that this was all new to him. But he didn't look afraid as he walked unhesitatingly into the darkness and was swallowed by the black space. As he disappeared she hurried after him, not wanting to be separated, and barely noticed the instant of blindness as she crossed through the Door Between Worlds.

The Villagers had accepted their decision to leave with equanimity but once it was decided, Zoë felt almost reluctant to go. Over the past week this place had become familiar and she wasn't looking forward to stepping through the blackness of the Door into an uncertain future. Wandering out through Katryn's garden on to the hillside she breathed in deeply, trying to savour what might be her last taste of fresh air for a while.

She was about to go back inside when a moving figure attracted her attention and she turned to see Taryn the herber gathering sheaves of long grass still wet with the morning dew.

'I hear from your friends that you'll be leaving us soon,' the old woman said. Her manner tended to be curt with all of the world-travellers, despite the fact that she had helped them.

'That's right,' Zoë nodded. 'Thank you for all your help. I really appreciate it.'

'That's more than Alex does,' Taryn said sharply. 'Since he obviously intends to get himself sliced up again as soon as possible.' Zoë didn't know what to say but Taryn went on after a moment, 'Your Laura's a different sort of problem.'

'I think it was magic that did it,' Zoë said hesitantly and Taryn's eyes snapped at her.

'It was evil that did it,' she said definitively. 'And there's more than one sort of healing required there. But whatever it takes is beyond my skill.'

Zoë waited, certain that the old woman was going to say something more and eventually Taryn turned to regard her with a narrow look.

'You don't understand our life here, do you?' she said.

'Um . . . not really,' Zoë admitted, trying to think of a polite way to explain herself. 'It's true I don't understand why you don't seem to relate to the Door at all. I mean, it's just across the river and there's the orchard around it but no one ever mentions it and if we do people just don't seem interested.' She blushed a bit at what she was saying but began to feel almost annoyed. 'I just don't understand,' she repeated feebly and Taryn scrutinized her.

'No, you don't,' she agreed. 'Your Alex doesn't either. I've had questions for a week about everything under the sun. One day he's asking if we know how to dig for metals in the earth, or grind flour in a mill. The next it's about how we govern ourselves and if we trade with our neighbours for things we cannot make here and do we use tokens of currency or barter for goods. Your Jhezra was at it as well yesterday when I stopped in for a word with Katryn, although she actually asked about something sensible for a change.'

'What was that?' Zoë asked, seeing that she was expected to, and Taryn grinned at her suddenly.

'Medicines, what do you think? And I've put aside for her what I can spare although you'll have to read the instructions, unless you want to go poisoning yourselves.'

'Thank you,' Zoë said gratefully and then went on slowly, 'I am truly grateful to your Village for letting us stay here. It's a really beautiful place even if . . . '

'We don't achieve all that much?' Taryn's eyes gleamed brightly with amusement before she turned to look towards the dipping hills and valleys stretching off towards the horizon.

When the herber looked back at Zoë there was a difference in her expression and after a moment she said drily, 'Achievement can be measured in a number of ways. I'll tell you a riddle, Zoë. If you travelled all the way around our world back to this point you would find no settlement larger than a village and no people who do not live by the same philosophy as we do here. What do you think of that?'

'I suppose that is a kind of achievement,' Zoë began then she stopped speaking, thinking of something, and she could feel her eyes widening as she stared up at Taryn. 'The whole world?' she asked in surprise. 'Everyone lives this way?'

'You guess it, then?' Taryn's eyes snapped with satisfaction. 'Our civilization may seem simple to you but it's the way the entirety of the people agreed to take.'

'Then were things different once?' Zoë said, unable to hold back her curiosity. 'Did you have cities and mines . . . and wars?'

Taryn stepped back into the field and picked up her basket of grasses. It was clear she'd said all she was going to and Zoë hung back for a moment before calling a goodbye and the old woman nodded at her.

'Safe travelling, then,' she said with an air of finality and Zoë waved at her before going back indoors.

Kal kept his hand on the hilt of his sword as his world vanished behind him and blinked at the sudden change of light. He'd been wary even before he'd taken the final step through the Door and he'd entered the Library prepared for almost anything. It was something of a shock to discover that the twins had been telling the truth about what awaited them.

He was standing in a shadowy corridor, shelved on either side with multiple rows of books, illuminated by the pale glow of mage-lights hanging from the low ceiling. The corridor was long and wide and slightly curved, receding into the distance in both directions without ever deviating from the repeating pattern of the endless bookshelves.

Turning to look back at the Door he saw Morgan standing behind him and looking around wide-eyed at the scene that surrounded them.

'Welcome to the Great Library,' Charm said and Ciren at her side added:

'And to the community of world-travellers. Now you are both truly members of the Collegiate.'

'I never imagined so many books,' Morgan said, still staring about her.

'They are of many different types,' Ciren said, leading the way down the corridor with a smooth stride. 'Some have been brought from libraries of the various worlds.' He gestured at the shelves on either side and added to Kal: 'These here are from your world. Books about the history and geography of the Tetrarchate lands, their customs and culture, their skills and resources.'

'In this section of the Library we try to make certain that the books pertain to their nearest Doors,' Charm said, breaking easily into the conversation. She and Ciren seemed relaxed, walking down the corridor in step with each other. 'You've seen that we keep a journal of our travels. Sections of that which describe the Tetrarchate may end up being shelved here. Some of these books are diaries of other travellers who came to your world many years ago.'

Kal stopped at that and looked more closely at the rows of books. Taken individually they lost their homogeneity and he saw that they were made of differing materials and of a variety of sizes. The twins didn't object as he took one down from the shelves and opened it, carrying it closer to the nearest light source to read the words. Translation magic was spelled into the Archon's crown and he had no difficulty making out the title which took up most of the first page: *Being a Catalogue of the Flora and Fauna present on the Principal Continent of the world called sometimes the Patchwork of Cities or the Thousand Kingdoms: from a study by Febrifruge the Botanist using the ordering system of Clavius the Patterner.*

Kal turned the pages carefully, studying the neat lines of text marching down the pages interspersed with painstaking illustrations of the petals of flowers or the digestive systems of animals, exquisitely rendered in coloured inks.

'Is that the kind of thing you write in your book?' Morgan asked, looking over Kal's shoulder at the text and then turning back to the twins. 'I've seen you drawing maps.'

'Maps can be crucial,' Ciren said. 'Travelling through Doors is so simple that it's easy to forget that worlds themselves are vast expanses and you may have to travel many miles before finding a Door. Or even travel that long and not find one. If we didn't map our travels we'd be in danger of losing our way.'

'But with worlds that have been explored earlier it's possible to use information from the books others have written,' Charm added. 'So what we write is about the subjects which most concern us.'

'And what most concerns you about my world?' Kal asked, wondering if the twins would answer. But Ciren didn't seem at all reluctant to speak.

'When we first came to your world we became suspicious that the Hajhim were being supported by an other-world group. We returned for more direct evidence of the nature of that support.' He looked at Morgan as he continued. 'Thanks to you, we have the names of those responsible and someone who can describe the world they come from. That was the object of our mission.'

Morgan blanched at that and Kal frowned, although he didn't speak. Ciren and Charm might be prepared to reveal more now that they were actually in the Library but Kal was still conscious that nothing had yet been said about the mysterious Wheel. But he didn't think it was wise to voice too many of his suspicions just yet. Keeping his thoughts to himself, he returned the book of *Flora and Fauna* to the shelf it had come from and allowed the twins to set the pace again down the corridor.

When Zoë went back to the blacksmith's forge Dynan was sitting at his workbench reading a thick leather-bound book. She hadn't meant to disturb him but he shut the book as she came in and smiled at her.

'So you leave us today, Zoë?' he said and she nodded. Dynan was a quiet man and she knew Alex thought he was a little slow from the way that it always took him a long time to reply to anything. But Zoë noticed that although there were a couple of older men in the Village who were treated very respectfully, both those men had a habit of talking quietly to Dynan in the forge at night.

'Thank you for your hospitality,' she said politely and when Dynan nodded she waited, feeling certain he was going to tell her something.

'Your friend Alex was here the other day,' the blacksmith said, looking at her calmly over the closed book. 'He asked me if I could make him a sword.'

'Oh,' Zoë said. And then when Dynan said nothing she added: 'I expect you told him you couldn't.'

'That's right.' A broad grin spread gradually over the blacksmith's face. 'Has anyone ever told you how sensible you are, Zoë?'

'Only my dad,' she found herself answering and then had to swallow the lump in her throat.

Dynan looked troubled and then he glanced down at the book he was holding before meeting Zoë's eyes.

'I expect you're hoping for some sort of advice,' he said abruptly. 'To take with you on your travels.'

'Yes,' Zoë said, meeting his eyes sincerely. 'Can you help me at all?'

'I don't know,' the blacksmith frowned. 'Any advice I might give you could be as easily good as bad but I can't rightly let you leave without telling you something.'

He paused for a long time and then sighed and began again. 'You'll find beyond that Door that there are many rules you haven't heard of and don't understand. It's important to remember that no one else understands them either. You'll find that there are many different kinds of people but I think you already know that people have more in common than they lack.' He looked away for a long time and Zoë thought he'd finished when he spoke for the third time.

'The wisest man I met was someone called Caravaggion of Mandarel. It was he who taught me the folly of ever giving advice. If you're as sensible as you seem I hope one day you'll understand why I haven't told you any more than this.'

'I hope so too,' Zoë said eventually when she realized there wasn't going to be any more than that. 'But you have been very kind. I won't forget it.'

'And we won't forget you,' Dynan told her and he rose to clasp her hands in farewell. 'I'll find Katryn, so she can say goodbye,' he told her and went up the backstairs to the upper level of the house.

Zoë glanced once at the closed leather-bound book still lying on the workbench before taking a step back. Putting her hands firmly into the pockets of her army coat she went into the kitchen to look for Jhezra.

Morgan had always liked libraries. At school she tried to avoid the screaming hordes in the playground and used to sneak back in to hide herself behind the shelves of books. Her favourite stories were fantasy fiction, tales of elves and dragons and quests, but she would read almost anything that allowed her to escape the reality of her own mundane life.

The Great Library inspired her with a sense of awe. The hugeness of it, the endless winding corridors, the Doors open to hundreds of new worlds and the vast collection of books on every subject imaginable was overwhelming. As they'd passed through the shadowy corridors she saw the black and red Wheel symbol recurring over and over again. Sometimes it was painted where two corridors joined, occasionally it was carved into the wood of the shelves and increasingly it appeared on the spines of the books that surrounded them. But the Wheel was most oppressively present as insignia on the clothing of the people they passed: men armed with swords who stood silently posted along the corridors and plainly dressed people selecting books from the shelves who turned to watch them as they passed by. Ciren and Charm had spoken to one of these men, who had gone along ahead of them, and Morgan realized that wherever they were going their arrival wouldn't come as a surprise.

The long corridor had developed a very gradual slope downwards and, as she followed Ciren and Charm's lead, Morgan fought against a tendency to drag her feet. This was all going too fast for her and she looked at Kal with relief that there was someone who found all of this as strange as she did. But Kal's face was cold and distant, his grey eyes screening his thoughts, as he looked expressionlessly ahead. The Archon's crown sparkled in the light of the floating light-globes and the slim rapier he carried glinted at his hip.

Pulling herself together Morgan raised her chin defiantly as a nearby guard's eyes lingered on her for a few extra seconds. Back in Shattershard she'd walked through the city with the same air of disinterest, pretending to herself that she was older and more powerful. Smoothing back her long black hair behind her ears Morgan glanced at her bitten fingernails before hiding her hands in the sleeves of her black tunic-dress. Remember you're a magician, she told herself, trying to calm her fluttering heartbeat.

The corridor took a final twist and headed for a T-junction ahead where two more silent guards stood on either side of an archway leading into a darkened room. As Charm and Ciren arrived the guards bowed, stepping back to give them room to pass through.

'This is the Chamber of the Wheel,' Ciren said quietly, taking his place at Charm's side. 'This is where you'll find your answers.'

* * *

After saying goodbye to the blacksmith's family, Jhezra took the lead as they left the Village and set off down the road to the Door.

'I know we need to find a magician who can cure Laura's blindness,' Zoë was saying, walking in the centre of the group with Laura holding on to her right arm. 'But I think our priority should be to find a way back home.'

'Back to Earth?' Alex asked, sounding surprised. 'Won't that be impossible?'

'How should I know?' Zoë said. 'But I never wanted to leave Earth for good.' Her voice sounded choked as she added, 'My dad must be so worried . . . he won't have any idea what's happened to me. And what about your parents? They must be frantic.'

'I somehow doubt it,' Laura said, coolly. 'They've never been interested in anything that's happened to us so far.'

'You can't mean that, surely?' Zoë looked shocked and she turned to Alex for confirmation. 'Don't you want to go home?'

'Not especially.' Alex shrugged. 'To be honest I liked the desert much better.' His eyes met Jhezra's, holding a warmth that hadn't been there for a while. 'I felt more at home with the Hajhim than I ever did on Earth.'

'But many of my people were killed during our assault on Shattershard,' Jhezra said slowly, meeting his eyes with a frown. 'And more still must have died when the city fell. Who knows how many or how few survived. Perhaps none.'

Alex looked away, his face tightening, but Zoë looked distressed and she said quietly, 'Perhaps some survived.' She looked seriously at Jhezra. 'If we can find a way, do you want to go back and look for them?'

Jhezra thought about that for a while, as they walked through the meadow towards the orchard. She'd promised to help Zoë get home, feeling responsible for the collapse that had cut off the other girl from everything she knew. She hadn't expected that Zoë would offer the same service in return.

'If it were possible, I would want to know what happened to my people,' she said. 'But any of the Hajhim who survived would be at the mercy of the Tetrarchate now. If I returned I would want to bring them a new hope for survival. Perhaps there's something in another world that could help them.'

'I bet there's a million things,' Alex said suddenly and his eyes were alight again as he looked over at her. 'The mistake we made before was underestimating the Tetrarchate. Just in the last week, I've thought of lots of things we should have done. We should have had cellphones to co-ordinate the attack, and night-vision goggles and proper guns as well. If we'd just brought one Hajhi war-band into Weybridge we could have taken all kinds of things from the army base . . . '

'No, you bloody well couldn't!' Zoë's expression was outraged. 'Weybridge Garrison isn't a toy shop . . . you can't smash and take guns just like that . . . and the army aren't toy soldiers either. You'd have been shot!' She shook her head in contempt, stepping away from Laura as she did so, and turning to look at Alex and then Jhezra. 'What's wrong with you?' she demanded. 'Can't you think about anything except war?'

Jhezra looked down, bowing her head as she felt the truth of what Zoë was saying. Alex's use of outlandish weapons had ended in tragedy once already, and with the best intentions Jhezra's advice to her people had brought about their destruction. But Laura wasn't quelled.

'If you hadn't been under our protection you would have found Shattershard a much less pleasant place,' she said softly. 'As Jhezra can tell you, the Tetrarchate weren't exactly benign.'

'But starting a war didn't help, did it?' Zoë demanded hotly. 'Maybe things weren't perfect there but they got worse after you interfered . . . You were so sure you were right . . . but you didn't know as much as you thought you did and that's why the city was destroyed.' Her voice was hoarse with the effort of reining in her feelings as she finished: 'These worlds are real places . . . and we can't act as if this is a game . . . it's not right.'

'I don't think of it as a game,' Laura said coolly. 'But you must admit that you . . . that *we* know very little about other worlds. Certainly we have no idea how to set about finding a route back to Earth or to the Tetrarchate world.'

'I know,' Zoë admitted and Alex curled his lip scornfully.

'Zoë led us out of Shattershard,' Jhezra said suddenly. 'We were in the dark then and she found us a way out. I think we should trust her.' She met Zoë's eyes, trying to show the other girl that she was willing to follow her lead, and Zoë smiled hesitantly.

'Trust isn't the issue,' Laura said smoothly. 'I hope we can all agree to get along, whatever our aims are. But we need a more detailed plan than simply looking through every Door we pass.'

'Then we ought to find someone who can tell us about the Library,' Zoë said eventually. 'About the worlds and the Doors and the Collegiate and all the other things we don't really know anything about. Laura's right that it would be crazy to just wander from world to world without any idea of what's out there or how dangerous it could be. We need to find a guide, someone who knows more about the universe than we do.'

'So the plan is for Zoë to lead the way while we look for some kind of guide?' Alex asked. 'And try to find out what this Collegiate is all about.'

'That's right,' Laura said and her mouth curved in a

thin smile. 'Although I suspect it's a case of the blind leading the blind.'

As the four teenagers disappeared behind the trees of the orchard, Katryn waved a final goodbye and headed back to her kitchen, leaving Dynan and Taryn standing alone on the bridge.

'And so it continues,' the blacksmith said wearily. 'Four more innocent travellers strewing chaos in their wake.'

'Innocent?' The herber snorted with laughter. 'They are not children like your Averly. They are almost adults in knowledge and apprehension, and they came to us with the marks of war and violence still upon them.'

'The universe is a dangerous place,' Dynan pointed out and his mother shrugged.

'So will it ever be as long as people prize power over peace.'

Dynan nodded. 'Still,' he said, 'I wish we could have told them more.' He glanced back at the forge building, thinking of a large leather-bound book inscribed with pages of his own careful handwriting. 'Hazards out in the worlds tend to be obvious, the dangers of the Library are more subtle.'

'The greatest threat they face is the one they themselves pose,' Taryn said in gentler tones. 'That is a lesson that cannot be taught. They will have to learn it, as we did, by making their own mistakes.'

5

The Chamber of the Wheel was cast into shadow by the low lamplight. Books with red and black bindings ringed the walls and as Morgan followed Kal and the twins through the entrance she saw the wide round table with its spoked wheel design before she noticed the figures seated in the heavy wooden chairs that surrounded it in a semi-circle.

There were eight of them, all men, and in the shadows she could only just make out their faces, shrouded in robes or hooded by cloaks. On the left hand edge of the semi-circle one of the seated figures looked up as they entered. He was a grey-haired man with wire-framed spectacles and he poised a quill pen above a book before him as he spoke:

'I declare this Council in session. The order of business is the return of the twin agents Ciren and Charm.'

On the other side of the table a man with grizzled features fiddled impatiently with a pen, flipping the slender instrument back and forth like a baton between his large thick fingers.

'How fared the mission,' he asked abruptly. 'And who are these new people that you bring among us?'

'Golconda Moraine.' Ciren bowed politely to the seated councillor. 'We have returned with the information that was required and these, our companions, are proof of the fact.'

'Then do not delay,' a papery voice said softly from the back of the table and Morgan moved close to Kal as the shadowy figure raised its head to regard them. 'Let us have your report.'

The twins had taken up a formal position in front of the table with Morgan and Kal slightly behind them and now Ciren turned slightly towards them as he spoke.

'Allow me to introduce Kal and Morgan. Kal was previously the Archon of Shattershard and Morgan is a world-traveller from a world named Earth.'

'Greetings,' Kal said, with a gesture of his head and Morgan tried to smile as she met the eyes of the man with spectacles.

'Welcome to the Library,' he said, looking first at Kal and then at her, his hand travelling methodically across the pages of the book in front of him. 'I am Periphrast Diabasis, Secretary of the Wheel. These others here are members of our faction's Council.' His eyes were small and pebble-like behind the lenses of his spectacles and they looked Morgan up and down thoughtfully before returning to the twins.

'Our companions know little of the Collegiate and nothing of its factions,' Ciren said, with a glance back at them before returning his attention to the Council. 'We have come at considerable speed from the ruins of Shattershard lately destroyed through the activities of a group of uninitiated world-travellers.'

There was movement among the councillors as some of them leaned into the light. They were old and the low light carved wrinkles and furrows across their faces. From the darkest shadows behind the table the most distant figure did not move but a withered ancient voice said:

'Deliver your report.'

'We proceeded as per instructions to the borderland of the Tetrarchate,' Charm began and the councillors leaned back expectantly. 'There we entered the city of Shattershard searching for the reasons for the increased trouble with the nomadic tribes of the Hajhim.'

'As we had postulated an other-world influence was supporting the Hajhim,' Ciren continued. 'But the source was two world-travellers named Alex and Laura Harrell who had entered the city through a nearby Door from the world of Earth.' He gestured briefly at Morgan and added: 'Morgan is also from that world but had no hand in the disturbance and was living and working as a mage in the city at the time.'

'We discovered her identity as a world-traveller,' Charm said and Morgan remembered just how easy that had been for the mind-reading mage. 'Then we made ourselves known to her as Collegiate members and began to initiate her in the codes of the Collegiate.'

Following on from her words Ciren spoke again to add:

'In return she shared information with us about the Harrells and even attempted to dissuade them from interfering in the local politics, using as her intermediary a younger girl who had been brought through the Door by them recently.'

The man who had introduced himself as Periphrast Diabasis looked over at Morgan again but he said nothing and Charm continued.

'We had travelled to the area in the company of a Tetrarchate troop,' Charm continued. 'The commander of this troop declared martial law, in effect overriding the authority of Kal, the city's Archon.'

There was another movement around the table and Kal stood still and straight under the councillors' attention, waiting for the twins to finish their explanation.

'Kal at this time had formed a relationship with Morgan,' Ciren said softly and Morgan blushed and looked at the floor as he continued. 'And although she hadn't told him about the role of the Harrells he was beginning to suspect influences behind the Hajhim.' He paused in his recitation for a moment and seemed to hesitate about what to say. 'Our concern at this time was to contact the Harrells ourselves and make known to them the existence of the Collegiate. However, matters quickly escalated beyond our control.'

'The tribes had been equipped with a form of other-world weaponry using the explosion of brimstone devices unfamiliar to us,' Charm explained. 'Using or misusing this they managed to trigger a series of earthquakes in the caves beneath the city which resulted in its complete destruction.'

'This occurred at the height of the battle,' Ciren concluded. 'We encountered Morgan and the Archon and were obliged to convey them to safety but we were unable to salvage the Harrells.' He stopped speaking and Charm waited a moment before adding:

'The destruction of the city effectively isolated the Archon from his world and he elected to travel with us and Morgan to the capital city. There we thought it advisable to bring him through to the Library.'

Silence fell and Morgan tried to swallow away the dryness in her throat. These old men were like a board of examiners who knew about a hundred times more than she did about everything. It was Periphrast, the secretary, who eventually spoke:

'We thank you for your report,' he said and Ciren and Charm both stepped aside from the table, leaving Morgan feeling suddenly exposed to the watching Council. 'Morgan and Kal . . . ' He paused abruptly and then looked narrowly at Kal: 'Or do you prefer Archon as a term of address?'

'My status is gone with my city,' Kal said, not smiling but keeping his voice soft and smooth. 'I'm content to be known by my name.'

'Indeed.'

It was impossible for Morgan to read the secretary's expression as his pen scratched a few characters across his book but then his head angled in her direction and she said uncertainly, 'I'm just Morgan.'

'Those of us who inhabit this section of the Great Library are known as the faction of the Wheel.' The secretary's thin fingers drummed suddenly on the surface of the table. 'You will learn more about us in due course. For now we offer you the hospitality of our faction.'

He turned towards Ciren and Charm and they stepped forward obediently as he said, 'Ciren and Charm, you will be held responsible for Kal and Morgan while they remain within our territory.'

As she followed the gradually curving corridor of the Library, Zoë tried to suppress her feeling of annoyance with Laura. The other girl's blindness didn't seem to have made her at all humble; she accepted Zoë's arm as if she was owed it and she listened mostly in silence to her descriptions of the branching corridors they passed through.

Laura's fingers held on lightly to her sleeve but Zoë felt as trapped as if they'd been roped together. She hadn't asked for any of this and now she didn't have any choice but to accept it, but all the same she felt as if she needed a break from the crippling weight of Laura's reliance upon her.

'Alex,' she said suddenly, 'can you help Laura along for a little bit, please? I want to have a look ahead.'

Alex looked as if he would have liked to object but Laura was his sister after all and in the circumstances he could hardly complain. Laura stopped walking immediately but she said nothing as Alex fumbled for her hand.

'I'll scout ahead with you,' Jhezra offered spontaneously. 'If that's all right, Zoë?'

'That's fine,' Zoë told her, feeling a bit embarrassed by her outburst now that everyone was reshuffled into the places she had dictated for them.

But as the group started walking again she felt immediately more comfortable and she turned to Jhezra with a smile.

'I'm sorry I lost my temper earlier,' she said. 'Sometimes this all gets a bit too much for me.'

'I'm sorry if I think too much of war,' Jhezra said quietly, looking at her with liquid dark eyes. 'But the Hajhim have suffered a long time under the yoke of the Tetrarchate and struggle has always been a part of my life.'

'Well, it's not as if we'd outgrown war back on Earth,' Zoë told her. 'My father's a soldier, you know. A major.' She stopped and laughed at herself. 'I suppose that doesn't really translate,' she said.

'No, I can understand that,' Jhezra said to her surprise. 'A high rank among warriors, a leader of others to war, is that right?'

'Yes, sort of,' Zoë told her. 'But he doesn't actually go to war. He just makes sure that our bases are prepared for various eventualities.'

'Your country has been at peace for a while then?' Jhezra asked and paused to glance back at Alex for a moment. 'Alexander told me some things about your wars and about the soldier Lawrence.'

'Lawrence of Arabia?' Zoë thought back for a little while and then said: 'Dad said something about him before I left Earth . . . That . . . that Lawrence was more of a hero than a soldier because the British army never forgave him for going native.' She bit her lip, remembering her last quiet night at home with her dad before adding, 'I remember something else,' she said. 'Dad said that we were all products of our own culture no matter how hard we tried to see another point of view.'

Jhezra was silent for a while as they walked along together and lost in her memories Zoë was startled when the other girl finally spoke.

'I had a friend,' she said. 'Vaysha. You met her once in the desert, remember?' When Zoë nodded she went on. 'Well, Vaysha was a true fighter. Our people have a training exercise called shadow dancing, a fight you make with your own shadow, and of all of us Vaysha was always the most skilled. She was ferocious in battle also and she hated the Tetrarchate and the people who lived in Shattershard with great passion . . . But when Alexander first came to our people he sold books, some about how to make weapons or how to make war but others about all kinds of things. Vaysha bought almost everything he could bring. She told me once that reading those books was like having a window into another world where everything, even what she thought about things, was different.' Jhezra looked across at Zoë and her eyes sparkled with wetness. 'But she said that when she stopped reading the window closed and she was back in the desert and it was as if nothing had changed.'

'That's terrible,' Zoë said, meeting Jhezra's eyes helplessly. 'I don't know what to say . . . except that at least Vaysha had a glimpse of another world . . . that's something, I suppose . . . '

'We at least have more than a glimpse,' Jhezra said, her mouth twisting into an almost smile. 'We are here,' she gestured at the shelves that hemmed them in, 'surrounded by books, although I cannot read them, and surrounded by worlds, although I do not understand them . . . But perhaps we can find something here that will make a difference . . . so that when we go home it won't be as if nothing has changed.'

'That's true,' Zoë agreed. 'I mean look at all these books! It's like all the knowledge in the universe . . . it must be able to teach us something we can use to make things better.'

Morgan sat nervously on the edge of a hard wooden chair while Kal paced around the room. After their brief introduction in the Chamber of the Wheel, the twins had brought them here and told them to wait. Presumably the councillors of the Wheel were deciding what to do with them and Morgan wondered what they would decide. When Ciren and Charm had explained who they were the group of old men clustered around the circular table had barely looked at them, leaving her to feel like excess baggage brought back through customs.

Like all the other parts of the Library they'd seen the twins' room had bookshelves extending from floor to ceiling on every wall. But someone had rigged up long curtain poles along the sides of the room so that thick black drapes could be drawn across to hide the books and turn the room into a dark tent-like interior instead. At the end of one wall the room was T-shaped and two beds, partly concealed by more curtains, took up the corner space. Other than that the only furnishings were chairs and a couch, a desk, and a couple of wooden chests.

Searching for a distraction she looked up at Kal, who was still exploring the room, and smiled nervously.

'So what do you think of all this?' she asked.

'I'm still deciding,' he said slowly, a strangely troubled expression on his face. 'What do you think?'

'I'm not sure,' Morgan admitted. 'But all these people are from different worlds, aren't they? It stands to reason they'd be a bit strange to us.'

'You're not strange to me,' Kal pointed out, tweaking a strand of her hair, and Morgan blushed.

'I'm glad you're here,' she said. 'Sometimes, in all this, I don't feel as if I know who I am any more.'

'You're not the only one.' Sitting on the side of her chair Kal put an arm around her comfortingly. 'But I'm glad you're here too.'

'It hasn't turned out so badly has it?' Morgan said thoughtfully, leaning into Kal's chest. 'The Library's amazing . . . all these books . . . and the Wheel seem to be all right, don't they?'

'They've been very polite,' Kal said, his voice sounding strange but when she looked up he shrugged at her. 'I'm reserving judgement until we've found out some more about the Collegiate,' he said easily. 'The Secretary of the Wheel did say we'd find out more in due course.'

'And maybe Ciren and Charm will explain more too,' Morgan suggested.

'Perhaps,' Kal agreed. Getting up from the arm of the chair he looked round the room thoughtfully. 'But the more I discover about the twins the stranger they seem.' He glanced back at Morgan and went on, 'It's not just that they're magicians, all their responses are unnatural somehow . . .'

'I know what you mean,' Morgan agreed. 'It's strange, isn't it? Maybe it's something to do with being twins; it's as if they're two halves of the same person.'

'No.' Kal shook his head. 'It's more than that.' He frowned and fell silent again for a moment before finishing slowly, 'There's something inhuman about them.'

Laura's fingers rested lightly on her brother's arm, keeping just enough contact for her to catch hold if she stumbled or let go if he faltered. She'd already realized that Alex was hopeless at leading the way. Zoë had made a much better guide-dog, even if she had pointed out complete irrelevancies like the colour of flowers and shade of leaves, at least she didn't cause Laura to keep tripping over things because she'd forgotten to mention them.

But aside from the occasional odd twist to their route dictated by Zoë and Jhezra up ahead or a pile of books left scattered on the floor that Alex hadn't thought to point out, there was a definite pattern to the Library. Laura could feel the gradient of the corridors changing gradually, sloping up or down as they walked, although the floor beneath her feet was seamlessly smooth. She knew that they curved as well from the way that Alex would jostle against her unexpectedly from one side or another despite her attempts to follow a straight line.

In her head Laura was forming a picture of the route they'd taken, something like an underground map, with Doors as stations along the bending lines of the Library corridors. But the spatial relationships were confused by the way the corridors rose and fell and she wondered if the Library could be a hollow world, with the corridors radiating around a sphere. It was annoying not to know more about gravity or astronomy, she thought with a flash of irritation, and she was wondering if Alex might know any more than her when he spoke suddenly.

'So what do you think about this idea of Zoë's?' he asked, dropping his voice importantly. 'Finding someone to teach us about the world-travelling, I mean.'

Laura listened to the low murmur of voices up ahead before she answered. From the fragments she'd overheard earlier the two other girls had been swapping stories about their worlds and now they seemed to have moved on to a discussion about books. It was almost sweet really the way they were going through their own little making-friends rituals and she wondered if Alex had noticed that Jhezra was barely speaking to him nowadays.

'Well, Zoë certainly knows more about it than we do,' Laura said eventually. 'Morgan seems to have told her all sorts of things . . . ' She paused, counting things up in her head. 'About there being a Door under the city and about this Library and also about the Collegiate, this organization of world-travellers she'd joined.'

'Morgan really lucked out, didn't she?' Alex replied with a sudden burst of bitterness. 'Our whole plan gets messed up and we get buried alive under the city, me with a busted arm and you blind. Meanwhile she gets a huge magical power-up and joins the world-travellers' Club Med.' He huffed out a breath and added: 'I bet she escaped the city too, don't you?'

'Probably.'

'You must really hate her,' Alex said after a moment and Laura's fingers twitched for a second against his sleeve.

'I suppose,' she said vaguely, to make him drop the subject.

It sounded as if Alex was actually jealous of Morgan, she thought, trying to collect her thoughts. It was incredible really. Morgan Michaels had been such a typical Goth-type back on Earth. She'd even had something of a crush on Alex in her shy stammering way. Growing up in Weybridge among the same group of kids from infant school to GCSEs Morgan had always been on the edge of things. It was the fact that she used to wander around in the woods behind Bicken Hill that had brought her to Laura's attention and she and Alex had sometimes met her in the woods behind the garden. That had led them to the Door and to Shattershard and there Morgan had lapsed into a Goth girl's fantasy, first getting treated by everyone as a mage and then finding out that she actually did have some kind of magical power.

That was where Morgan had really lucked out, Laura decided, forget the rest of it. It was magic that had given her the edge as a world-traveller and it was magic that had blinded Laura. Laura's fingers twitched again and she suppressed a frown as she thought about it. In a universe where magic existed how were you supposed to cope with it? Morgan's magic had made her blind and Morgan had probably meant it to leave her dead.

Laura's fingers twitched again in a burst of irritation. She'd never really believed in Morgan's magic, dismissing it as conjuring tricks; certainly she'd never had any inkling that Morgan could command real power. To Laura power was in politics, in the machinations and manipulations of courtiers and merchants, or perhaps in armies or war-bands. It seemed somehow undignified that the other worlds should contain such a clichéd fantasy concept as magical powers, and deeply unjust that Morgan should suddenly gain what must have been her favourite daydream.

Alex swerved into her again from the side and Laura compensated automatically, adding a bend in her mental underground map. Perhaps there were other worlds like

Earth without magic, or worlds where magicians were as common as bricklayers. Perhaps magic was something you could learn like algebra or astronomy. Or maybe magicians could be hired like bodyguards to protect you from magic users who tried to harm you.

However it worked there must be rules, Laura told herself. Everything had rules, down to the physics of the universe, otherwise it would just fly apart and there would be chaos.

Ciren and Charm waited outside the Chamber of the Wheel for the Council meeting to end. It was certain that their patron, Vespertine Chalcedony, would have additional instructions now that they'd delivered their report. But as they waited Ciren was aware of a sense of unease.

Kal and Morgan's introduction to the Wheel had gone well but the situation was still new to him. In their years of travelling the worlds this was the first time they'd actually initiated a world-traveller into the Collegiate and he was conscious of feeling responsible for the newcomers. The Wheel might keep to the rules of the Collegiate in public but in practice their mode of operation was a bit more complicated. In particular they took the rule of non-interference in other cultures very loosely indeed.

Vespertine Chalcedony, their patron and the Founder of the Wheel, had a passion for organization and as a result the faction encouraged any world they discovered to form united societies in which everything was recorded and regulated. Although they hadn't planned it the destruction of Shattershard was a help to them, disposing of the rebellious Hajhim and the independent city-dwellers, but Morgan and Kal presented an awkward problem.

For a start Morgan's insistence on bringing Kal with

them was, strictly speaking, breaking the Collegiate rule against telling natives about Doors. Then Kal was fiercely independent and his immunity to Charm's mind-reading ability meant that the Wheel would be cautious about him. Ironically Laura and Alex Harrell might have fitted into the Wheel much better. Although all Collegiate members were bound to disapprove officially of such dramatic interference in another culture, the Wheel attempted a similar thing at a more subtle level.

Ciren only hoped that the Wheel would think Morgan's magic and Kal's intelligence useful enough to bring them into the faction's secrets. Until then he feared that the two newcomers would not feel comfortable in the Library. His eyes met Charm's across the corridor and he moved closer to ask her quietly, 'What do you think it means for us to be responsible for Morgan and Kal?'

Zoë could have cried when the first person they'd met in the Library took one look at them and turned round and ran away.

'Stop!' she called out and although the stranger kept going, Jhezra leapt into action at once. Chasing after the stranger with long flowing strides that ate up the distance easily, she seized hold of the newcomer and dragged him back over his protests.

'Please, don't hurt me!' he said, trembling with terror as Jhezra marched him back down the corridor. 'I'm unarmed.'

He certainly didn't look as if he could pose much of a threat to anyone. He was a boy, a man really, Zoë supposed, a little older than Alex, with greasy looking long hair and anxious brown eyes. He was dressed in a peculiar assortment of clothes that looked like nothing more than a selection from the Oxfam bargain bin: a rusty orange woollen jumper that came down to his bony knees and a pair of battered leather trousers. He'd stopped struggling and was looking pleadingly at Jhezra.

'Don't hurt me,' he said again, quaking in his boots, and Zoë felt bad.

'We won't hurt you,' she assured him. 'Jhezra, let him go.'

Jhezra released the collar of the stranger's jumper and stepped back, raising her hands in a gesture of openness before bowing slightly.

'I'm sorry to have troubled you,' she said politely. 'My name is Jhezra.'

Unlike the people in the Village the young man seemed to have no difficulty understanding her and, pulling himself together, he straightened his rumpled clothing in a dignified way and said, 'All right then, I'm Glossali Intergrade, member of the Cult of the Catalogue.' He gestured at the surrounding bookshelves and continued, 'We're based in this section of the Library. Who are you and what do you want?'

'I'm Alex Harrell,' Alex said asserting himself abruptly as he and Laura joined them. 'This is my sister Laura.' He looked towards Zoë and she didn't wait for him to introduce her.

'My name's Zoë,' she said. 'And we're sorry to have disturbed you. We just wanted to . . . ' she paused, trying to work out how to explain it and saw Alex shift at her side. She didn't wait for him to begin his own explanation of who they were and what they were doing. 'We only wanted to ask for directions,' she said.

6

When Glossali Intergrade had recovered from his initial fright he was willing enough to be friendly.

'I was just on my way to the refectory,' he told Zoë and the others. 'And I'm sure you must be hungry after your travels. Please, do follow me . . . '

The refectory turned out to be a long low room furnished with plain wooden tables and chairs which had a large cauldron-like pot standing on a trivet at one end of the room. It was half full of a lumpy brown porridge which Glossali poured carefully into wooden bowls and served to them. To be honest Zoë would have preferred the bread and cheese Katryn had packed for them but it seemed rude to refuse when the young Catalogue Cultist was being so generous and she accepted her bowl politely.

The porridge had a strange meaty flavour overlaying a coarse grained texture and Zoë found it tough going. Alex didn't eat much of his and Laura had only one spoonful before saying she wasn't hungry. Without comment Jhezra took Laura's bowl and finished it as cleanly as she had her own.

'All the Catalogue Cultists eat here,' Glossali Intergrade explained as a group of other people arrived while they were eating and served themselves, sitting down to eat at seats further down the long table. 'We have studies and dormitories around and about this section.'

'So what is the Catalogue Cult?' Zoë asked and Glossali's pallid face brightened up as he looked at her.

'It's a very exciting development in Collegiate factions,' he said enthusiastically, dripping porridge on his orange jumper as he gesticulated with his spoon. 'We're originally an offshoot of the Scholars but our interests are a lot more specific . . . '

'Excuse me,' Laura's voice said softly and Glossali broke off in mid-sentence to look at her.

Despite her blindness Laura's head was turned in Glossali's direction and it was almost possible to believe her light green eyes were focused on him.

'I'm sorry to interrupt,' she said politely. 'But could you go back a bit. I didn't quite understand what you meant by Collegiate factions.'

'You didn't?' Glossali looked puzzled for a moment and Zoë felt she had to explain.

'We're very new to world-travelling—' she began but Laura interrupted her.

'And don't know much about Collegiate history,' she said smoothly. 'We'd be grateful if you could explain it.'

'All right then, I'll go back to the beginning,' Glossali said willingly, obviously happy to lecture. 'Although all members of the Collegiate are expected to obey similar rules, laid down in law-books and codes and bibles throughout the Library, we all have different ideas and objectives. Some people go travelling off through the Doors, exploring worlds and suchlike.' He gave a dismissive waggle of his spoon. 'But inside the Library we're broken up into factions based on the sections we occupy or the work we're interested in doing.' He looked up and down the table at them as if checking they were keeping up and Alex nodded a little impatiently.

'What work do you do here?' Jhezra asked curiously and Glossali looked a bit miffed.

'Well, organizing and cataloguing and listing books for a start,' he said. 'So that people who come through the Library can find what they're looking for. And trading with other factions for information or with agents out in the worlds to supply us with resources.' He pointed up at the cauldron of porridge at the end of the room and added: 'We import everything we need, you see, food from one of the local Doors, paper and inks from another Door, sometimes we trade with the nearby sections for books.' He paused to take a breath and said ponderously: 'And then there's the central purpose of the Catalogue Cult.'

They waited while Glossali pushed his bowl out of the way and steepled his hands in front of him on the table as he explained.

'You see the Great Library is very large,' he began. 'There are a number of theories about exactly how large it may be, but suffice to say that it contains millions upon millions of books. Now . . . ' Here his expression became very serious and he lowered his voice to emphasize the gravity of what he was about to say. 'None of these books are arranged in any consistent order. Obviously the more responsible factions organize their sections according to their own scheme but there are empty sections and abandoned sections and most of the books just lie about any which way all over the shelves.'

'We read some books earlier,' Zoë said nodding, 'and we couldn't make out if they were even fact or fiction.'

'Exactly!' Glossali agreed, taking up the thread of his

lecture again. 'And this naturally presents a problem to any dedicated seeker after knowledge. Therefore there are certain Collegiate members who have made it their life's work to compose catalogues: indexes, listings, and bibliographies of the various sections to aid in searching through the stacks . . . '

'And that's what you do?' Alex asked with an edge of incredulity.

'No, no, you must be patient.' Glossali looked a bit annoyed at the interruption. 'You see, these catalogues on their own are useless. Imagine one catalogue for every hundred books, well that's ten for every thousand, and ten thousand for every million . . . far too many to be easily searched. So there are other writers who compile catalogues of catalogues, describing each one by where it was last seen in the Library and what sort of books it lists, much more useful, I'm sure you can see.'

'Um, yes,' said Zoë slowly. 'So you make catalogues of catalogues then?'

'No,' Glossali shook his head. 'We collect them.' He beamed with pride in response to her dazed expression. 'You see why it's such an exciting development? We collect catalogues of catalogues and also catalogues of catalogues of catalogues. Almost any book in the Library can be found with the help of our catalogues!'

Zoë had to look away to conceal her grin. It was clear that he thought his work a great accomplishment but she had it worked out differently. The Catalogue Cultists might have collected thousands of books but not one of them was of any immediate use. All they could do was tell you where to look for a catalogue which would list where to find another catalogue which might tell you where to look for the kind of book you originally wanted.

'That's very impressive,' a voice said smoothly and Zoë looked up in surprise to see Laura looking at Glossali with an expression of warm sincerity. 'I wonder, would you be willing to show us around your section some more?'

It wasn't until the other councillors had left that Vespertine Chalcedony summoned Ciren and Charm back into the Chamber of the Wheel. Too old and frail to move easily from his great chair he didn't move as they entered but his dry papery voice whispered to them from across the room.

'Come closer, my children. Come and show me your book.'

Charm didn't hesitate, walking around the table to place the book before their patron as she took the seat on his right-hand side. Ciren mirrored her movements to slip into the chair on Vespertine Chalcedony's left. With a sigh of satisfaction the ancient councillor rested his hands on the smooth black and red leather binding.

'Did you enjoy your travels?' he asked before opening it, his deep-set eyes regarding the twins with avuncular interest.

'The new world is congenial,' Charm told him. 'It's not surprising the only resistance to Tetrarchate rule came from the inhospitable borderlands. The rest of the citizens seem to be prosperous and content.'

'The Hajhim seemed to prefer their independence to the Tetrarchate's prosperity,' Ciren said uncertainly.

'There are always those who resist rational organization,' Vespertine reminded them, his voice whispering almost as softly as the pages of the twins' book. Opening the cover he turned methodically to the place in their journal where they had arrived in Shattershard, his thin wrinkled fingers tracing the route of the journey they had faithfully mapped.

As the ancient councillor read the chronicle of their travels, Ciren looked down at it himself, the neatly written script and carefully sketched maps and scenery carrying him back to the city of Shattershard.

'Of course, it's all gone now,' he said abruptly, as Vespertine brooded over a meticulous drawing of the city's walls and towers. 'There's nothing left of Shattershard but rubble.'

'Something always survives,' Vespertine said, not raising his eyes from the book as he turned the page to regard a portrait of Kal wearing the Archon's crown. Underneath Ciren read his own words describing what they had guessed about the crown's powers and felt uncomfortable as Vespertine lingered over the page. 'You cannot read him?' the councillor said, his voice rasping drily as he focused his penetrating gaze on Charm.

'No.' Charm's mouth tightened in an expression of frustration. 'And Ciren couldn't place the nature of the crown's magic. It's something new.'

'Another lesson, my children,' Vespertine said still staring down at the crown. 'Very little is new.' He leaned back in his great chair so he could look at them both, leaving the book open on the table before them. 'Consider the Doors, we do not create them, we discover them. Therefore each new world we discover has already been found once before . . . ' His voice drifted out across the table, the thin whisper of sound losing itself in the expanse of the room, as he told them: 'The universe is very old.'

Leaning back over the book Vespertine continued to read the story of their encounters with Kal and with Morgan, the account of the battle and their escape from the collapsing city. It wasn't until the regular lines of script in the twins' identical handwriting came to an end that he spoke again.

'I see that you dissuaded Kal from discarding the device,' he said at last, looking curiously at Ciren. 'And that you permitted Morgan to tell her lover about the Collegiate.'

'I've read that rule has been often broken,' Ciren said uncomfortably. 'And the crown seemed too powerful to casually discard.'

'You are correct not to wish it to pass out of our influence,' Vespertine agreed slowly. 'But it presents us with a difficulty.' His head swung back to Charm as he asked: 'You've read the girl, what does she think of us so far?'

'Morgan is curious about how the Wheel stands in relation to the rest of the Collegiate,' Charm replied instantly. 'And she is awed by the dimensions and extent of the Library itself. But her primary concern is with her own magic. She loves it but since her attack on the Harrell girl she fears it as well.'

'Interesting . . . ' Vespertine's dry voice betrayed a hint of pleasure at that. 'We shall have to discover more about the nature of her magic and persuade her to put it to use for us.' He paused and looked back to Ciren before adding: 'And what of the boy, without being able to read him, how do you assess his state of mind?'

'I think he's honourable, by his own lights,' Ciren said slowly. 'But his aristocratic upbringing has made him fiercely independent. I don't know what he will make of the Collegiate . . . or of the Wheel.'

'But I can read him through Morgan,' Charm added quickly. 'She loves him passionately and they have no secrets from each other. As long as he tells her everything he thinks, there's no need for concern.'

'Good.' Vespertine nodded approvingly. 'You are learning subtlety in exercising your power,' he told Charm. But Ciren wondered if what Charm had said was really true.

'Morgan has told him Charm can read minds,' he said carefully. 'If he guesses she cannot read his . . . '

'You must be circumspect,' Vespertine told them. 'I cannot imagine anyone better suited to watch over these two new initiates than you, my children. Even without being able to read Kal's mind, you will doubtless have several opportunities to gauge his opinions, and I will have two of the councillors arrange to see them as well.'

'But what if they don't want to join the Wheel?' Ciren asked and heard a plaintive note in his own voice.

Vespertine looked at him and Ciren felt his doubts dissolve in the face of the councillor's composed presence.

'Then you will persuade them,' the councillor said and the twins bowed their heads in silent assent.

Zoë wandered vaguely up and down the long lines of bookshelves. After the peculiar porridge meal Glossali Intergrade had taken them further into Catalogue Cultist territory to show them some of the books his faction collected. Zoë and Alex searched the shelves looking doubtfully at the catalogues of catalogues while the others followed behind. With Laura's blindness and Jhezra's lack of a translation device there wasn't much point in them looking at the books.

Zoë was beginning to think that there wasn't much point in her looking at them either but Glossali had shown them through the section with such pride that she didn't really feel able to insult him by saying so. Instead she tried to ask him about the other factions he had mentioned as they walked.

'So how many factions are there in the Collegiate?' she asked. 'What kinds of things do they do?'

'No one knows how many there are, just as we don't know how far the Library truly extends,' he told her, looking around at the neatly shelved books with satisfaction as he strolled along at her side. 'Each faction has their own aims and interests. Scholars study books, Cryptographers make up languages, Nominates give things names, Perigrinades travel the worlds, Jurists keep up the ancient customs of the Collegiate.' He made a vague gesture down the corridor. 'Those are just some of the factions we trade with though, our catalogues have references to many more. Would you like to see a catalogue of catalogues of lists of the factions?'

'Thank you, no,' Zoë said hurriedly. 'Can you tell me more about the customs of the Collegiate. You mentioned rules earlier . . . '

'Yes.' Glossali frowned at her. 'But you must know the rules if you're members of the Collegiate, surely?'

'Well, we kind of stumbled into the Library by accident,' she explained uncomfortably. 'There's a lot we don't know.'

'I see.' Glossali thought for a moment. 'Well, every faction interprets the rules a bit differently. There's a lot of debate about what they really mean. But one of the most important is that Collegiate members are expected to help and forbidden to harm each other.'

'OK,' Zoë said thoughtfully. 'Go on . . . '

'We must identify ourselves as world-travellers using standard recognition symbols,' Glossali went on, ticking off points on his fingers as he recited them. 'And lead uninitiated world-travellers to the Library. But we may not reveal the existence of the Collegiate or the Doors to natives. And it's not permitted to use knowledge from one world to influence another.'

Zoë glanced back at the others and discovered that Alex was still scrutinizing the bookshelves on the other side of the corridor but his back was tense and his head tilted slightly to listen to them. Jhezra was more obvious in her interest, watching Glossali with bright curious eyes, and Laura, standing nearby, had turned her head in their direction.

'Who does not permit this?' Jhezra asked abruptly and Glossali looked puzzled.

'Everyone,' he said frowning and Alex turned to join their conversation.

'I think what Jhezra means is, who enforces these laws?' he tried to explain and Glossali brushed away his clarification.

'They are ancient traditions,' he said, with an air of pride. 'Whatever happens in the worlds, Collegiate members obey the laws of the Library.'

'But how can you know what's going on outside the Library?' Zoë pointed out. 'If you stay in here . . . um . . . cataloguing all the time?'

'Peregrinades bring news from outside,' Glossali said, looking uninterested. 'So do Booksellers and Mapmakers. But our work is more important than keeping up with mere local gossip.'

'I see . . . ' Zoë said, considering. Obviously Glossali wasn't even interested in any world beyond that of the Library and wasn't much interested in the Library beyond his own small section. She wondered if there was anything he could usefully tell them at all.

Alex had turned back to look at the books but he had a small scornful smile on his face and Zoë guessed he had come to the same sort of conclusions as she had. Jhezra looked thoughtful but didn't say anything and it was left to Laura to finally speak.

'So,' she said, her eyes distant as she turned her head towards Glossali. 'If we, as world-travellers, need your help you will simply provide it to us?'

'Well, of course,' Glossali agreed and then added: 'If I can, and if it isn't dangerous.'

'Oh, it isn't dangerous,' Laura assured him and her expression lightened into a smile for the first time Zoë could remember in ages. 'As you can see we're uneducated in your customs and at present we are looking for someone to give us advice. Perhaps you could direct us to a person or a faction who can teach us more about the laws of the Library?' She paused and then moved her head slightly, so that she was speaking more in Zoë's direction. 'That was what you wanted, wasn't it?' she asked politely.

'Yes,' Zoë agreed, wondering why Laura was suddenly being so helpful; but she didn't have time to worry about it as she looked back at Glossali. 'Maybe those Jurists you mentioned,' she said. 'Perhaps they could help us learn more about the Library?'

Glossali hesitated, his gaze shifting from Jhezra's sword to Alex's smirk, to Laura's unseeing eyes, before returning to Zoë.

'Well . . . ' he said slowly, drawing the word out while he thought. 'I suppose I could take you to Jurist territory, it's not that far away.' He chewed on one of his fingernails absentmindedly for a moment before continuing more enthusiastically, 'And there's probably some errand I can run for the Catalogue Cult while I take you there . . . '

'We'd appreciate it very much,' Laura said gently, her eyes still distant and watchful as they waited for Glossali to commit himself. 'And perhaps you could explain some more about the Catalogue Cult as we travel?'

'Yes, I could certainly do that,' Glossali agreed, looking cheerful at the prospect. 'All right then, consider me your guide.'

'Thank you!' Zoë said fervently, and she heard Jhezra and Alex echo her words. But Laura didn't say anything, smiling to herself as if listening to music only she could hear.

* * *

When Vespertine Chalcedony dismissed them the twins took a circuitous route back to their room. It wasn't unusual for them to do so. Often their patron's orders required discussion and interpretation and walking through the corridors of the Library gave them an opportunity to gauge the mood of the rest of the Wheel.

However, this time as they wound their way through the stacks it was a while before either of them spoke.

'He didn't seem to think it would be difficult for us to persuade Kal and Morgan to join us,' Ciren said eventually.

'And although you have argued the same thing throughout our journey now you seem doubtful,' Charm said and the sharpness in her voice caught Ciren by surprise.

'And you, despite insisting he was dangerous before, told Vespertine Chalcedony that you weren't concerned,' Ciren pointed out and Charm's stride faltered for a moment as she looked across at him.

'What did you expect I would say?' she asked suddenly. 'That I wouldn't back you up? That I would tell him we had disagreed?'

Ciren stopped walking and met Charm's eyes, the dark purple orbs that mirrored his exactly, the expression of hurt in a face he knew better than his own.

'Maybe,' he said slowly, feeling again the force of the disconnection that had put them out of step with each other. 'Perhaps just disagreeing once has changed things between us.'

'It's you who've changed,' Charm said immediately. 'I haven't. It's you who won't tell me what you're thinking any more.' Her thin eyebrows drew together in a perplexed frown. 'Vespertine Chalcedony thinks Kal presents a problem for my mind-reading but it's the barrier that's grown up between us that's really blocking me. I don't understand why you're different now . . . you never were before.'

'I know,' Ciren admitted, feeling a strange doubt in himself.

For as far back as he could remember he and Charm had always been each other's other half. They'd grown up together at the centre of the Wheel firstly as adopted wards of Vespertine Chalcedony and subsequently as his agents. Reading books from a thousand cultures, they'd been taught by a succession of Collegiate members how best to use their unique talents to benefit the Wheel. In all that time Ciren had never doubted that the Wheel was right in its interpretation of the Collegiate's code, that its influence over their worlds was good or that their patron was benevolent. As long as he was certain of himself and his twin everything else seemed perfectly natural.

Now Ciren realized that his certainty had been weakened: from the moment he'd first been puzzled by his twin to her reciprocal confusion about him now. After fifteen years they'd finally begun to question what they knew about each other.

'It was the existence of the Archon's crown that made me start thinking,' he said out loud, admitting what had first caused the rift between them. 'It made me wonder what it was like to be you, how it had affected you to be able to read anyone's mind, now that for the first time you couldn't.'

'That's what you didn't want me to know?' Charm frowned. 'I still don't understand. Why couldn't you just tell me that?'

'Because . . . ' As he spoke Ciren realized that he was finally putting into words something he'd always shied away from admitting. 'Because it's not the crown that's unusual . . . it's us. There are no other people like us. I've never heard of a mage who can read minds as you do or sense magic as I do. It's not natural to any world we've ever heard of. It's not a normal thing to grow up with.' He wondered if his face showed the desperation he suddenly felt as he stared into the black-purple tunnels of his reflected eyes. 'I didn't want you to know I thought we were different.'

Charm's pale pointed face shifted strangely into an expression halfway between a frown and a smile as if she was genuinely uncertain of what she felt.

'I didn't know you hadn't realized,' she said. 'I've always thought we were different. There's me and you . . . and then there's everyone else. Hasn't it always been that way?'

'But if we're so different from other people . . . ' Ciren said slowly, 'what are we?'

Alone in her personal darkness Laura had trained herself not to fumble like an invalid. At least the corridors of the Library followed the same basic design so that she didn't have to grope along the walls or shuffle slowly across the floor. But while Alex and Zoë were able to look at the volumes of books and read the signs that their guide pointed out to them, she was left out and had to follow along behind.

However she wasn't the only one left out. Jhezra was unable to read the books either and since Glossali was still cautious of her she too trailed behind at the back of their little group. Ahead Laura could hear Glossali's somewhat sententious voice informing them of this and that, intercut with sarcastic remarks from Alex and polite responses from Zoë. Laura didn't need her vision to see them clearly in her mind's eye. But Jhezra, walking quietly beside her, presented more of an enigma.

Directing her attention towards where she thought the other girl was, Laura tried to imagine her face. Jhezra was attractive to look at, she remembered; Alex had liked her from the outset of their adventures in the Tetrarchate world. She was tall and lean and never went anywhere without her scimitar and sickle-shaped dagger. Her eyes were dark brown set underneath dark brows, her mouth was wide with white teeth and her face mobile, quick to frown or laugh. Back in her own world she had worn the typical clothes of the Hajhim, sand-coloured like the desert, but Laura remembered from something Zoë had said that she had been given a white linen shirt in the Village because her own was torn.

Laura thought of Jhezra as an essentially simple person, focused on work and on war, her life led outside and far away from civilization. Compared to the rest of them, educated on Earth, Jhezra was an anomaly in the group.

'You don't seem to spend much time with Alex any more,' Laura said and sensed a sudden movement as if her words had startled Jhezra.

'That's true,' the Hajhi girl replied, drawing the words out slowly as if she wasn't sure what she was admitting to.

'I know he misses you,' Laura lied. Actually she wondered if Alex had got tired of his barbarian warrior-girl when his dream of being Lawrence of Arabia had collapsed around his ears. But she was sure he wouldn't mind having a girlfriend on hand if Jhezra was amenable to the idea.

'There's been so much change recently,' Jhezra was saying. 'It's a lot to adjust to, and Alexander was almost as badly injured in the earthquake as you were.'

'It wasn't the earthquake that did this to me, it was Morgan,' Laura said sharply before she remembered to get back to the central point. 'But anyway, it's been hard for all of us . . . But now that things are more stable perhaps the two of you should talk?'

There was silence for a while and Laura could guess what Jhezra wasn't saying. She'd be annoyed at what she'd see as interference in her business and feel awkward that it was Laura who'd brought up the subject rather than Alex himself. All the same though she would also be flattered and concerned by the idea that Alex had missed her and in the end the result was completely predictable. Jhezra would have to talk to Alex now, she wouldn't be able to help herself, and after that it would be in his hands.

It was a pity that Alex would almost certainly undo her good work, not seeing the advantage of having the only armed member of their group as a loyal follower rather than a reluctant ally. But at any rate it was worth a try and, if Alex failed, there were other options. Laura's attention drifted back to Glossali as she considered possibilities. Weakness was a kind of strength as well.

Left to wait in the twins' room Kal felt tense and on edge. What made it worse was having to keep his feelings hidden from Morgan. She was nervous herself and having to reassure her went against the grain for him. But he didn't have any choice.

Ever since he'd learnt Charm could read Morgan's mind any time she wanted, Kal had played a dangerous game. He'd had his suspicions about the twins even back on his own world and those unformed doubts had solidified when he met the Council of the Wheel. He'd tried to speak politely to the councillors but he had seen at a glance what kind of people they were: old men, hoarding power and knowledge for themselves, hiding behind the letter of the law. What Kal had feared about the Library had come to pass. He'd escaped from the influence of the Tetrarchate only to fall into the hands of a group just like them and the Wheel had powers and knowledge the Tetrarch had never dreamt of.

But he couldn't let Morgan know his real feelings. Kal might view the Wheel with deep suspicion and distrust but Morgan couldn't be allowed to know it. If Charm were to read her mind and find evidence of Kal's doubts they might both be in danger. It was all very well for the twins to say that Collegiate members were forbidden to harm each other, no one even knew that Morgan and Kal were in the Library except the Wheel. So Kal had to lie by omission and keep his fears secret, and the fact that he was doing it to protect them both didn't make his task any easier.

In the end he'd distracted Morgan by commenting on the books that shelved the room, books bound in every conceivable colour and style; volumes of philosophy, warfare, and magic. One long shelf held a run of books bound in wildly dissimilar styles and Kal was surprised to see that the spines all bore the name of the same author.

'Look at this,' he said, idly, taking one of the books down and flipping through it. 'All of these are by someone called Caravaggion of Mandarel.' As Morgan came to join him Kal scanned down a paragraph and then read out loud: *'Where Doors appear interests clash.'* He raised his eyebrows at Morgan for her reaction but she had taken down another of the Caravaggion books and read out a paragraph herself:

'Give me a man who breaks a rule over one who bends one. When something is broken others can see the harm that has been

done, but if it is merely bent the damage cannot be seen until another trusts his weight to it.'

'Interesting,' Kal said, putting his own books back thoughtfully. 'Is this Caravaggion a priest, do you think?'

'It doesn't say,' Morgan said, shrugging. 'I wonder which of the twins these belong to?'

'I would guess Ciren,' Kal told her, replacing the book in its place on the shelf.

'How come?' Morgan asked curiously and he had to bite his tongue to stop himself answering automatically. Saying that Ciren seemed the more intelligent of the twins wouldn't exactly endear him to Charm.

'It was just a thought,' he said casually, and turned away from the bookshelves to put his arms around Morgan's waist.

Instantly responsive she returned the embrace and Kal felt a pang of guilt as he bent his head to kiss her.

'You know,' she said, after a moment. 'I can think of better ways to spend our time than just waiting for the twins to come back.' She blushed a bit as she smiled up at him but her green eyes glinted at him and Kal laughed softly.

'I think we can, at that,' he agreed.

7

Alex flicked through the pages of another useless book and ground his teeth in annoyance. Back when he and Laura had been trading items from Earth to the world of the Tetrarchate he'd brought through a fair few books himself: mostly martial arts manuals and books on the history and philosophy of warfare. Although he wasn't much of a reader himself, he'd actually got quite good at anticipating the interests of his customers and was proud of his ability to guess how useful or relevant a book would be from the title and only a few pages of text.

If this section was at all representative, the books of the Library were almost entirely useless. They had paused at a junction of corridors at the edge of the faction's control for Glossali to go and speak to one of his superiors in the Catalogue Cult. While the others waited, Alex had followed Glossali's directions to a cramped cupboard where a bucket with a lid served the function of a toilet. When he'd found out that there wasn't even any toilet paper Alex hadn't hesitated to tear out a few pages from the book he was carrying. As far as he was concerned it might as well be good for something.

Shoving the remains of the book back on to an empty space on the nearest shelf, Alex walked back to where he'd left the others, head craned to scan the titles on the shelves as he passed by. It wasn't beyond the boundaries of possibility that something here might be useful. Something that could lead him to books about weapons or magic or the science of world-travelling, for example, would be extraordinarily useful. However, he'd stopped really believing that he would find anything like that.

The idea of a Great Library was all very well, he thought to himself, but what this place basically needed was some organization. Shaking his head at a set of engraved plates of fossilized fish, he looked up and saw Jhezra walking down the corridor towards him.

'Hey,' he said, feeling pleased, and shoved the book back at random on to the nearest shelf. 'How's it going?'

'I wish I had thought to purchase a translation charm back in Shattershard,' Jhezra said, regretfully, running a hand gently across a line of books. 'It makes me feel ignorant to be in the midst of so much learning and yet be unable to understand it.'

'Trust me, you're not missing anything,' Alex informed her. 'These people are cracked. There's nothing useful here.'

'Still, at least the Library is inhabited,' Jhezra pointed out. 'After our first wanderings here without food or water I feared the rest of it would be empty. But Glossali was as hospitable as the people in the Village.'

'I hope you're prepared in case we meet someone who isn't,' Alex pointed out, glancing at Jhezra's scimitar hanging from her hip. 'They can't all be so harmless.'

Jhezra looked thoughtful and Alex winced internally,

remembering how she'd caved in when Zoë had berated them for being fixated on war. All the same, he realized, if Jhezra had been truly convinced that Zoë was right surely she'd have stopped wearing weapons.

'You're the only one of us who can protect yourself at the moment,' he continued carefully. 'I lost my scimitar in the landslide and even if Laura wasn't blind she was never much of a hand at combat . . . ' He paused. 'And as for Zoë . . . '

'Yes, what of Zoë?' Jhezra's eyes fixed on him expectantly.

'Well, even though her dad is in the army she seems to be really pacifist, doesn't she?' he said. 'But she's still only a young girl, really. She seems much more naive than Laura, and this has all been a bit strange for her, hasn't it?'

'It's strange to me as well,' Jhezra replied. Her expression was troubled and Alex reached out to put a comforting hand on her shoulder.

'I am sorry about that,' he said honestly. 'Remember we talked about the differences between our worlds once? I never thought we'd both end up in one that was completely new to both of us.'

Jhezra nodded but her expression was distracted and Alex wondered if he should try to put his arm around her. It seemed like forever since they'd been alone together.

'You know,' he said after a while, 'I'm sorry I was so useless when we first found the Library. I think I was probably shell-shocked or something, I felt as if I was in a kind of a daze.'

'You were wounded,' Jhezra said and Alex nodded.

'Exactly,' he agreed. 'But I should have been more responsible. You and I have to look after the others.'

'According to Glossali Intergrade,' Jhezra said, pronouncing the unfamiliar name carefully, 'no world-traveller may harm another. Zoë seems capable of looking after herself.' She paused and added: 'And despite her blindness, so does Laura.'

Morgan and Kal were kissing when the twins eventually returned to their room. Lying together on the low sofa it was a moment before Morgan heard Ciren cough politely from the entrance and then she pulled away, blushing as she readjusted her clothes.

'Sorry to keep you waiting,' Charm said drily, as she followed her twin into the room and Morgan blushed again and looked away to cover her embarrassment.

'So what have your Council decided to do with us?' Kal asked, leaning back on his side of the sofa and not appearing at all flustered.

'You're to be offered every hospitality, of course,' Ciren said, hanging his cloak up on a peg and kicking off his boots with a natural ease that showed he considered this room home. 'Tomorrow someone will come to explain more about the Wheel and orient you in the customs of the Collegiate. Now that you're officially world-travellers it's important you know the laws of the Library.'

'So are we supposed to be members of the Wheel now?' Morgan asked. 'As well as the Collegiate?'

'Oh no,' Ciren shook his head. 'Not nearly. For now you are simply our guests.'

The twins seemed to be making a real effort to make them feel at home. While Ciren took a bottle of wine and a set of glasses out of a wooden chest, Charm laid out fresh linen and blankets on one of the curtained-off beds.

'I hope we won't be inconveniencing you,' Kal said politely and Ciren handed him a glass of wine hospitably.

'Charm and I are used to sharing,' he said and his twin nodded.

'Besides, the Council will be holding us responsible for you,' she added. 'We don't want you to have any reason to complain.'

All the same it was strange to be staying in this relatively ordinary room and know that beyond it there were the seemingly endless corridors of the Library and beyond that the mysterious Doors to millions of worlds. When there was a knock at the entrance a little later on Morgan looked up in surprise to see a man wearing a red and black Wheel badge carrying a tray of covered dishes. Ciren took it and thanked him and carried the tray over to the table, lifting the covers to reveal plates of appetizingly hot food.

'Where does it come from?' Morgan asked curiously and Ciren shrugged.

'Magic,' Charm said and Ciren smiled while Kal's eyebrows lifted in surprise.

'You have mages who can do that?' he enquired, taking his seat at the table. 'I've not heard of such an ability on my world.'

'Well, doubtless there are some mages who can create food,' Ciren said. 'But no, the food is real enough, we keep it in storerooms scattered throughout the section, but it's prepared and heated by a spell set by one of our mages.'

'It tastes real enough,' Morgan agreed appreciatively and nodded her thanks as Charm poured her another glass of wine. The Library was turning out to be much more luxurious than she'd expected and she tried to imagine what it would be like to belong here as the twins did, living and working among the Wheel.

Catching Kal's eye across the table she smiled as he raised his glass to her in a silent toast and wondered what he made of the Library so far. Unlike her he'd grown up in a world where magic was natural if not exactly commonplace, so perhaps this wasn't as strange to him as it was to her. But she wasn't sure how Kal would fit into a community of world-travellers. All his life he'd been destined to rule Shattershard and, even now the city was gone, with the Archon's crown gleaming in his golden hair Kal still seemed like a prince. Morgan was afraid he'd find it hard to adjust to life as an ordinary person.

Realizing what she was thinking she hid a smile. It showed how far she had come that she'd think of world-travellers as ordinary people. Maybe Kal wasn't a magician but he was bound to find a place for himself somewhere in the Library or maybe on another world, and Morgan forgot her food as she daydreamed about what the other worlds might be like and the life she and Kal could lead there together.

By the time Glossali Intergrade led them out of the Catalogue Cultist section, Zoë's head was swimming with everything she was learning. Back in the Village it would be about early evening, she guessed, but in the Library, with only the dim light of candles or torches, it felt more like the middle of the night. She had to keep herself from yawning as they made their way through the bookshelves.

Glossali led the way, consulting a map drawn across several pages of a book he carried, and Laura walked at his side apparently absorbed by the stream of explanations and qualifications the young Catalogue Cultist seemed to consider it his duty to deliver at every twist and turn of the corridors. Zoë followed after them wearily. She'd taken off her coat but it was awkward to carry under her arm and the rope of her kitbag dug painfully into her shoulder when she tried to sling it over that. Feeling low and tired she adjusted it again and tried to follow Glossali's endless travalogue.

Alex and Jhezra brought up the rear and Zoë had tried to tune out their conversation when she realized that Alex obviously wanted to talk privately with the warrior girl. His voice was low and intimate and Jhezra's replies even quieter still so that Zoë felt uncomfortable with the little she overheard. Really she supposed she ought to join Laura and their guide but right now she didn't feel she could take in any more information.

'Right, now we're coming to the Crossway,' Glossali was saying and he looked back over his shoulder at Zoë and the others as he added: 'I think you'll find this interesting. It's something of a landmark in this section of the Library.'

'Oh?' Zoë said, trying to infuse her voice with as much interest as she could and Glossali gave her a superior smile.

'Wait and see,' he said. 'I think you'll be impressed.'

After the multitude of wonders Glossali had pointed out so far Zoë rather doubted it but she lifted her head to look obediently and found herself looking up and up and up to a ceiling five times the height of the normal Library corridors and came to a stunned halt, trying to take it all in.

The Crossway was a vast room laid out in the shape of a cross. They had come in at the lowest level, the corridor widening out on either side just as the roof soared up above them, and on the other side of the wide expanse of floor she could see that it dropped back to its normal size at the other end of the room. Crossing in the other direction another corridor widened similarly to gigantic size to form the other branch of the cross before it too dropped back to its normal stature.

All around the sides of the Crossway the inevitable book-filled shelves stretched from floor to ceiling but with a difference. Built into the shelves every ten metres or so around the cross were staircases, leading up to balconies on each successive level and Zoë turned to see that above the corridor they had come from was another directly above it and another directly above that, the layers only made obvious by the great height of the room.

'It's amazing . . . ' she breathed, turning around again to try and take in the immensity of it.

'Unbelievable,' Alex said, coming forward to stare as well. 'Just how big *is* the Library?'

'All these are Collegiate members?' Jhezra asked and Zoë realized that the huge space of the Crossway was full of people.

They were everywhere, consulting books from the shelves, standing on the balconies, walking to and fro across the main floor of the room; dressed in a bewildering variety of styles and fashions and wearing tokens and patches that Zoë decided must be indicators of the faction they belonged to. Her gaze travelled here and there in the crowd picking out different designs and sigils. One man wore a shield-shaped patch depicting an open book; another group all had silvery stars pinned to their collars; three young women wore headscarves tasselled with gold coins; a tall man dressed all in black had a golden quill embroidered on the back of his long jacket; and another dodging nimbly through the crowds wore a green headband stamped with a white-winged horse.

Her eyes wide with amazement Zoë turned back to speak to Glossali and saw Laura standing still with an expression of patient expectance on her face, waiting to be told what they all were looking at.

'Sorry, Laura,' Zoë said automatically and started trying to explain what they were seeing. But it was too much to describe at once and Glossali took over the explanation.

'It's a true crossway,' he said. 'Because here we can access levels of the Library above us. The Jurist section lies higher up and this is the quickest way I know to get there.' He paused and then added: 'It's a good place to trade as well or to rest for a while.'

'I am rather tired,' Zoë admitted and to her surprise Laura turned towards her with an expression of sympathy.

'Let's stop and rest for a while then,' she said. 'If that's all right with our guide.'

'Oh certainly, certainly,' Glossali agreed. 'We've a way to go yet.'

'Thank you,' Zoë said fervently.

But as their guide led them to a place out of the main throng where they could dump their packs and bags, she couldn't help but wonder why Laura was suddenly being so nice to her again. Somehow it worried her, but she was exhausted and when she sat down beside the baggage she couldn't bring herself to care about anything except getting some sleep.

Charm had turned over her bed to Morgan and Kal after the meal and they had said goodnight early. From behind the drawn curtain she could hear muffled whispering so she knew they were still awake and while she doubted they were listening it was impossible for her to continue the conversation she'd begun earlier with her twin.

But Charm didn't mind waiting. Since they'd talked she felt at ease with her twin again, even if it was more a temporary truce than a real reconciliation. She'd been surprised to discover that Ciren was worried about how her mind-reading ability had affected her personality and she had wondered to herself if it frightened him that she could delve so easily into his private thoughts if she wanted to. But now that he'd trusted her she was content to wait and see what their next move should be.

'Can you recommend a book?' she asked quietly, and Ciren looked up at her and smiled.

'Of course,' he said, standing and joining her at the shelves. 'Didn't you say back in the Tetrarchate world you'd like to read something of Caravaggion's?'

'Yes, that would be interesting,' she agreed. 'Since you admire him so much.' She watched as Ciren chose a book for her and then one for himself before turning down the lamp to a low light for reading.

'I'm not sure that I admire Caravaggion exactly,' he said as he handed her the book he'd selected. 'I find his writing interesting but he's not always consistent. He'll eloquently argue one point of view throughout an entire book and then completely change his opinion in the next. It's hard to forget that even when he seems totally convinced by a concept he could abandon it utterly later.'

'What faction is he?' Charm asked and Ciren smiled wryly.

'There you have it,' he said. 'He's switched back and forth between many. He began as a native of the world of Mandarel. Then he was a Peregrinade for a long time, but he's also been a Bookseller, a Cryptographer, a Philanthropist, and a Scholar. It's impossible to pin him down to anything.'

'What is he now then?'

'I don't have his latest books,' Ciren admitted, 'so I can't be sure. But there was a rumour that he was involved with the Jurists not that long ago.'

Charm was silent for a while as she contemplated that. The Jurists weren't a faction she knew much about since the Wheel had little in common with them. She wondered if Vespertine Chalcedony would be likely to disapprove of Ciren's interest in someone from that faction.

'What are you reading now?' she said curiously, before beginning the book her twin had given her.

'Khelani's *Origin of Amulets,'* he told her and Charm raised her eyebrows.

'Hasn't that been debunked as a complete fantasy?' she asked and Ciren flashed her a quick smile.

'Yes, it has,' he agreed. 'But I still like it.'

Jhezra took a swig from her water bottle and carefully recapped it. One thing that worried her about the Library was that it had no obvious source of food or water; she hadn't forgotten those first few days wandering through the empty corridors and the habit of rationing water was ingrained into her from her upbringing in the desert.

Glancing to her side she smiled at the sleeping figure of Zoë, with her head pillowed on her bag and her face tightened into a frown amid a tangle of red-brown hair. Jhezra didn't feel tired yet herself; she was used to walking or riding long distances and had kept up her shadow-dancing exercises in the Village. But she remembered what Alex had been like when he first came to the desert, before he learnt to ride with the warriors and use a scimitar, and laughed to herself. Alex might pride himself on his skill at arms now but he had no call to belittle Zoë. She might be young and still weak but she had led them with courage and courtesy and now that she had dropped with exhaustion she took her rest like a warrior.

The others were exploring the expanse of the Crossway, but Jhezra had offered to look after their possessions and to guard Zoë's sleep. What the Harrells couldn't understand was that when Jhezra had accepted Zoë as her leader she'd made a commitment to the red-headed girl. She'd been brought up to be loyal to the war-leaders, not to follow them blindly when they stumbled into error, and right now Jhezra considered herself under Zoë's command.

'Strange that we should see things so differently,' she

mused to herself, watching Alex engaged in some sort of bargain with a stranger wearing a cloak covered in strange swirling designs.

Alex had made it clear that he was interested in resuming their relationship and although Jhezra couldn't help but feel flattered by the attention he was paying to her she was disturbed by it as well. His comments about Zoë had been casual enough but his implication that he would be a better leader came uncomfortably close to treachery to Jhezra's way of thinking. If you were dissatisfied with a leader's performance you might challenge them in public, but to sow seeds of disharmony behind their back was deceitful.

Jhezra shook her head, frowning. What Alex didn't realize was that not only was she uncomfortable with the idea of resuming their relationship, she was having grave doubts about having ever been involved with him in the first place. Alex's plan had led the Hajhim to death and disaster and Alex himself seemed untouched by it. It was true that at first he'd been shocked and disoriented but once in the Village he'd reverted to his old confident arrogant self. A man who craved power without accepting responsibility, who wanted to lead but lacked the courage to make a formal challenge, who wanted a sword when his hosts had sworn that he was safe, was not a man that Jhezra wanted as a lover.

She sighed and then started when she saw Alex walking back towards her. He was carrying something in his hand and he grinned at her cheerfully as he came up.

'Guess what . . . ' he began and Jhezra raised a hand in warning.

'Speak softly,' she said, setting action to words. 'Zoë sleeps yet.'

'Oh, sorry.' He lowered his voice. 'But I have something for you.' He held a clenched fist in front of her and chanted, 'Open your hands and close your eyes and you will get a small surprise.'

Jhezra hesitated, but Alex looked so happy and hopeful that she couldn't bring herself to disappoint him and she closed her eyes and cupped her hands in front of her. She felt a small hard object fall into them and opened her eyes to see Alex's wide grin before looking down at the thing he'd given her.

'A necklace?' she asked, looking at it. It was a metal coin of some description with bevelled edges and a hole bored through it near the edge through which was threaded a thin metal chain.

'It's a translation amulet,' Alex told her and his grin stretched wider at her start of pleased surprise. 'That chap over there was willing to trade me one for my watch. Don't worry, I tested it and it's legit . . . go on, put it on.'

'Thank you,' Jhezra said honestly, sliding the chain over her head and settling the coin around her neck. Glancing around for some way of testing the charm herself her eyes caught on the row of books on the nearby shelf and she blinked as the unfamiliar characters and symbols on the spines resolved into words she could read. 'Really, thank you,' she repeated, turning back to Alex. 'I'm more grateful than I can say.'

'My pleasure,' he said with a bow and Jhezra winced when she realized he would take her reply as encouragement.

But as Alex sat down beside her, Jhezra's eyes strayed to Zoë. Back in the Village the younger girl had sometimes gone to sleep early there too, tired out from the day's work, and every time she'd left her own amulet with Jhezra, pointing out with a smile that it wasn't much use to her while she slept. A true friend shared what they had without thinking about it, they didn't give you presents in the hope of your favour.

* * *

Morgan woke up in a sudden panic. Surrounded by silence and darkness she fumbled blindly about and felt the thick fabric of curtains all around her before a warm hand reached out and caught hers.

'Morgan?' Kal said fuzzily, sitting up beside her. 'What's wrong?'

'Kal . . . ' Turning into his embrace it was a few moments before she could speak and he stroked her hair, making soothing noises. 'It's nothing,' she said eventually. 'Just a bad dream.'

'What about, can you tell me?'

'No.' She shook her head. 'I'm not even sure now.' She hugged him back, feeling a bit more normal. 'I just know it scared me.'

Kal kissed the top of her head and stroked her hair again before drawing back the curtain that screened them off from the rest of the room. There was no sign of the twins but there was a decanter of water and another one marked wine placed obviously on the table next to a plate of flat breads. As Morgan climbed out of bed, pushing her hair out of her eyes and blinking sleepily, Kal crossed to the table and picked up a folded piece of paper lying there.

'They've left us a note,' he said, unfolding it. 'It says: *There's a washing room second right and first left down the corridor. You will be collected for orientation when the sand has fallen.*' He looked over at her with a puzzled expression. 'When the sand has fallen?' he repeated.

'There,' Morgan said, pointing out a device standing on a nearby shelf. It was a sand-timer filled with a glittery golden dust and, going over to check it, she saw that a third of the sand had already fallen from the top bulb into the bottom one. 'We had better get a move on,' she said.

'I think we had,' Kal agreed. 'Water or wine?'

'Just after getting up?' Morgan wrinkled her nose at him. 'Water, I think. Did you really drink so much back in Shattershard?'

'A fair amount,' Kal admitted, pouring her a glass of water before filling his own half full and adding a little of the wine to it. 'There was too much to think about, things I couldn't help or even influence, what with the Tetrarchate on one side and the Hajhim on the other. I used to drink a lot.'

'Well, I'll keep an eye on you,' Morgan said, half seriously, munching on a piece of bread. 'Since it looks like we're in a similar fix here.'

'Maybe for now,' Kal agreed, raising his glass to her. 'But if there's one thing that seems clear about this Library, it's that it has almost limitless possibilities. Perhaps once we've had this orientation or initiation or whatever, we'll be allowed to explore. And then . . . who knows what we might find.'

'That's what I was thinking last night!' Morgan exclaimed. 'That I'd like to explore . . . as long as we can stay together.'

'That's a given,' Kal told her, reaching out to touch her hand. 'I've no intention of letting us be separated.'

But that was what happened. Morgan finished first with the washing room and when she got back to the twins' room the last trickle of sand was dropping through the timer and an elderly man was standing there waiting for her.

'Morgan,' he said. 'You may recall me from your introduction to the Council of the Wheel. I am Periphrast Diabasis, Secretary of the Council.'

'Oh . . . um, pleased to meet you,' Morgan said uncertainly, conscious of her still wet hair, and wondered if she should offer to shake hands.

Periphrast Diabasis was tall and thin and swathed in thick black robes that fell with perfect smoothness to the floor. At first glance he looked bald but now she could tell his white hair was cropped close to his head and his flinty eyes regarded her narrowly through small round glasses. On one shoulder of his robe was embroidered the black and red symbol of the Wheel.

'Come with me now,' Periphrast ordered, turning to leave the room, and Morgan found herself moving after him before she remembered about Kal.

'Uh, Mr Diabasis, Kal's not back yet . . . should we wait?' she asked.

'Unnecessary,' the councillor informed her. 'His orientation will be conducted by another member of the Council.' A thin smile appeared briefly on his face. 'Do not be afraid. You will rejoin him shortly.'

There didn't seem to be anything more to say. Morgan wondered if Kal would have been able to insist that they stayed together in the face of this commanding person and she hoped fervently that what he had told her was true.

Periphrast Diabasis led her through several twists and turns of corridor before arriving at the entrance to the room that seemed to be their destination. Outside a man wearing the faction patch of the Wheel was standing guard but Periphrast didn't speak to him as he ushered Morgan inside.

'This is my study,' he explained. 'Take a seat.'

It was a bit like visiting the headmaster at school, Morgan thought, sliding into the hard wooden chair on one side of a large desk covered in neat piles of papers and books. Periphrast took the chair on the other side of the desk and steepled his hands in front of him as he regarded her for a long moment. Then he took a book from a nearby pile and opened it to a fresh page before dipping a quill pen in an inkwell and poising it to write.

'First,' he said, 'let's discuss the rules you've broken.'

8

Zoë woke with a sense of discomfort. Her neck was cricked from resting on her kitbag, her face felt grimy, and her eyes were crusted with sleeping dust. Sitting up, she looked around and was relieved to see Jhezra only a few feet away eating a golden-fruit.

'Good morning,' Jhezra said, with a smile. 'Or perhaps good day, since it's impossible to tell what the position of the sun is in here.'

'I expect it's morning somewhere,' Zoë said thoughtfully, rubbing the grit out of her eyes. 'Where are the others?'

'Alex is trying to bargain for a sword,' Jhezra said, gesturing somewhere across the room. 'But I think he will be unsuccessful. Only a few of the people I've seen carry any weapons at all and I doubt they'd sell one to a stranger.'

'I don't know why he even needs a sword,' Zoë began and then remembered Jhezra's own weapons and blushed.

Changing the subject to something less awkward she went on hurriedly: 'What about Laura and Glossali?'

Jhezra gave Zoë a shrewd look but didn't mention her lapse; instead she took another slightly withered golden-fruit from her pack and offered it to her.

'Our noble guide is comparing maps with some other travellers,' she said with a touch of amusement in her voice. 'As for Laura, she's been walking around and talking to people all over this place for some time.' She pointed again and this time Zoë turned to look.

Laura was standing on one of the balconies on the level above and to Zoë's surprise she was wearing a scarf tied across her eyes again. She was talking to a couple of women who seemed to be explaining something with much gesticulating and emphatic nods of the head.

'What is she up to?' Zoë wondered out loud and Jhezra met her eyes.

'Why, do you think she's doing something unwise?' she asked.

'No . . . ' Zoë said slowly and then shook her head. 'No, I'm probably worrying about nothing.' She sighed. 'It's just that since Shattershard I don't trust them,' she said. 'Laura or Alex.'

'Indeed,' Jhezra said and Zoë blushed again.

'I'm sorry,' she said instantly. 'I don't mean to be rude, I know you were involved with him . . . '

'Yes,' Jhezra admitted levelly. 'I was.'

Zoë felt embarrassed still as Jhezra finished the last of her golden-fruit, eating the seeds and core, and tried to busy herself with her kitbag. But after a moment of silence the Hajhi girl finally spoke.

'Have you ever had a lover, Zoë?'

'What?' Zoë's eyes met Jhezra's and then dropped again hastily. 'No, I haven't . . . Why do you ask?'

'You know that Alexander and I were together,' Jhezra began and Zoë nodded.

'I guessed,' she admitted. 'You two seemed very close.'

'I thought we were,' Jhezra said quietly. 'But I think now that I admired him too much. I believed . . . ' She paused for a moment and then began again. 'It isn't that he lied to me,' she said. 'I think he tried to be honest but it was as if he was playing a part. To him the desert was an adventure, and I don't think he ever understood that it wasn't that way for me.' She took another slow breath and Zoë listened, trying to understand what she was trying to say. 'Now the adventure is over and he wants to find another one. But my whole life is . . . not over but changed and Alex doesn't see that it must change things between us.'

Zoë thought about that for a little while and decided she understood how Jhezra was feeling.

'Do you blame him for what happened?' she asked carefully. 'For the destruction of Shattershard.' It took the other girl a while to answer.

'I don't see it the way you do,' she said. 'I never intended such chaos but it wasn't just the city that was destroyed . . . there was the collapse of all our plans. To take over the city, to fight the Tetrarchate, to rule the desert for ourselves. Alex made me believe we could accomplish all that and he was wrong.'

'So do you blame him?' Zoë asked again and Jhezra sighed.

'I know you do,' she said. 'What you said underneath the mountain, what you said when we left the Village, you blame him and Laura for involving themselves in our war, don't you?' Then, before Zoë could answer, she asked: 'Do you blame me as well?'

Zoë came alert at that, looking at the girl she'd come to think of as her friend across the heap of scattered baggage. She knew that Jhezra was trying to get at something and it was important how she answered but in all honesty she wasn't sure what she felt.

'God, Jhezra, I don't know,' she said at last. 'I don't have any basis for comparison. But . . . I guess I blame Alex and Laura because I don't think they should have interfered, especially by teaching you how to make bombs. Plus it was all selfishness anyway since they did it to make themselves important because if you'd won the battle they'd have been more powerful.' She took a deep breath. 'Although this is probably going to sound rude, I think I don't blame you because . . . they took advantage of you. Because they treated your world like a game.'

'Then you don't think I'm responsible at all?' Jhezra asked quietly and Zoë sighed.

'I don't know,' she said. 'Maybe a little. But I just don't know enough to judge you. I was only in Shattershard for a couple of days and in the desert for even less time than that. I don't know anything about the history of your conflict with the city or the Tetrarchate. I don't really know anything about you . . . but I'd like us to be friends.'

Jhezra didn't answer at once and, wondering if she'd said the wrong thing, Zoë wound her hands nervously in the fabric of her bag, waiting.

'I know only a little about you, Zoë,' Jhezra said finally. 'But I am honoured by you naming me your friend.'

'Well, I'm honoured to have you as one,' Zoë said, forcing a grin, and Jhezra smiled back.

Sitting facing Periphrast Diabasis over his huge desk, Morgan felt small and cowed. The secretary had questioned her thoroughly about everything she'd done since finding her first Door in the Weywode Forest, making copious notes throughout.

Morgan had quailed when he told her how many of

the things she had done were against the Code of the Collegiate. Despite her protests that Alex and Laura were responsible for the destruction of Shattershard he'd been disapproving when she admitted that she'd kept their identity secret from the twins until it was too late; he'd frowned over her admission that she'd stood with Kal on the palace walls against the Hajhim; and he'd fixed her with a long narrow look when she confessed to using a spell on Laura.

Periphrast Diabasis's pen looped and swirled across the page of his book as she completed her story.

'Then there remains the possibility that these others from your world,' he flipped back a page and read from his notes, 'Laura Harrell, Alex Harrell, and Zoë Kaul might have escaped the city.'

'I suppose,' Morgan said slowly. 'But it was a maze under the city, I don't think Zoë could have found the Door even if she could get to it under all that water. Kal wounded Alex badly in that last battle as well, you see. And I think . . . I think I might have killed Laura.'

Periphrast's glasses caught the light, concealing his expression as he looked at her, and Morgan stared at the floor.

'It was a dangerous breach of the code,' he said levelly and Morgan felt uneasy, looking back up at him with a sense of dread, but to her surprise his lips thinned in a gesture towards a smile. 'But I don't think we need worry about that in this case. After all, we don't even have a body, let alone witnesses. I think you may rest easy on that score.'

'But . . . but I don't even know what I did to her,' Morgan said, feeling shaken. 'I was angry and I wanted to hurt her but I don't know what spell it was I cast. I didn't even think I *could* do anything like that. What if it happens again?'

'That does present something of a conundrum,' Periphrast agreed affably, suddenly seeming more friendly. 'It's important that you be in control of your powers. We certainly don't want any more accidents.'

'Yes,' Morgan agreed, leaning forward eagerly. 'Can you teach me more about magic?'

'We will certainly endeavour to,' Periphrast said smoothly. 'We have mages among our number who will be able to advise you and I will provide you with some suitable books with which you may further your studies.' He made a note on a separate piece of paper before bestowing another smile on her. 'We have a saying in the Wheel . . . to achieve control there must first be comprehension.'

'OK,' Morgan agreed. 'That makes sense.'

She thought to herself that Periphrast was more like a headmaster than ever, now she was even being given homework; but it was a relief to know he took her magic seriously.

'Um, another thing, sir,' she said. 'I was wondering if we'd be allowed to explore some more of the Library . . . outside the Wheel area, I mean.'

'I don't imagine that will be a problem,' Periphrast said, glancing up at her. 'If you pursue your studies diligently I will arrange an excursion into the sections of our more friendly neighbours.' He smiled again at her expression of surprise. 'Not all of the Library is as safe as the Wheel.'

Laura walked carefully back down the staircase, running her fingers lightly along the handrail, but as she reached the ground a familiar voice sounded abruptly next to her.

'Oh hello,' Glossali Intergrade said. 'Would you like

me to escort you back to your companions? I believe they're preparing to move on.'

'Yes, thank you,' Laura agreed, stretching out a hand to take his arm. 'You're being very helpful.'

'Happy to do it,' the young Catalogue Cultist assured her. 'I must say, I'm impressed by the way you manage your disability . . . May I ask if you've always been blind?'

Laura hesitated. It wasn't a very tactful question but she'd already realized that Glossali wasn't a very subtle person.

'Well, no,' she said quietly. 'Actually I was hoping I might find someone who could cure me. You see I was attacked by a magician in one of the worlds we visited and what she did to me left me blind.'

'But that's horrible,' Glossali said and he did sound honestly appalled. 'I certainly hope we'll be able to find someone to heal you. Why did this mage attack you, do you know?'

'I can guess,' Laura said softly. 'She'd taken up with a group of natives and they were a fairly warlike lot.'

'But that's against all the laws of the Library and the Collegiate!' She could sense him gesticulating wildly as he tried to convey the enormity of his outrage. 'I assure you, Laura, you have no reason to fear this person. If they try to harm you here they'll be tried and punished; whatever section of the Library you're in, no one would permit such an atrocity.'

'Well, good then,' Laura said. 'You've been very reassuring.' She paused and then added: 'I'd be grateful if you didn't mention this to the others. I don't want them to know I was worried.'

'Of course,' Glossali pressed her hand. 'You can count on me,' he promised. 'And your feelings for your friends do you credit.'

'Thank you,' Laura said simply and, as she heard the voices of the others nearby, fell silent.

As the group gathered up their baggage and got under way, Laura kept her place beside Glossali. She suspected the Catalogue Cultist was beginning to feel protective about her and although she removed the scarf that bound her unseeing eyes, she took his offered arm willingly.

'Why were you wearing that scarf, Laura?' she heard Zoë ask curiously and she turned her face in the direction of the other girl's voice.

'Among so many strangers I didn't want them to walk into me, did I?' she said. 'It seemed a good idea to make it clear that I'm blind.'

'Oh.' Zoë sounded puzzled and Laura had to resist the urge to laugh. Poor Zoë might be as suspicious as she liked but it wasn't going to get her anywhere, she just wasn't clued up enough to guess what Laura was planning.

'Shall we go then?' Jhezra asked and Laura heard Alex sigh.

'I suppose so,' he said. 'But I wish I could have found someone to sell me a sword. This place seemed so promising.'

'At least you were able to find Jhezra a translation amulet,' Zoë pointed out cheerfully. 'And that's much more useful.'

'Not in the same way, it isn't,' Alex said grumpily and Laura felt a stab of annoyance.

'Nonetheless, I'm very grateful,' Jhezra said politely but Laura could tell the gesture hadn't accomplished any softening in the Hajhi girl's attitude towards her brother.

In fact as they set off Laura could hear that Jhezra had manoeuvred herself to walk alongside Zoë and Alex was left to trail along behind. It was really rather awkward the way Jhezra seemed to have bonded with Zoë but Laura didn't think the development was going to upset her plans.

Out in the worlds it would have been useful to have some kind of military support but in the Library Laura was beginning to feel perfectly capable of achieving her aims without any assistance. In fact as she listened to Alex whingeing once more about his lack of weaponry, she wondered if she might be better off on her own completely.

'It's dangerous out in the world, lad,' Golconda Moraine told Kal, striding along down a wide Library corridor. 'You wouldn't believe some of the things I've seen.'

'You said you were a soldier?' Kal asked politely, keeping pace smoothly with the grizzled councillor.

'That's right,' the older man nodded brusquely. 'Although this was a while ago, of course. The world I grew up on sounds a bit like yours, although I wasn't the ruler of a city.' He glanced at Kal's crown for a moment before going on. 'No, I was the third son of a country baron. Not a lot of opportunity out in the wilderness so I joined the army. Imagine my surprise in the middle of a campaign, we were chasing down some bandits I believe, to come smack bang through a Door.'

Kal made a noise of interest and wondered to himself what all this hearty man-to-man conversation was supposed to be accomplishing. He'd been concerned and then angry when he'd returned to the twins' room to find Morgan already gone and this Golconda Moraine had taken some effort to assure him that their separation was only temporary. Now the man seemed to be trying to bond with him over similarities in their experience. Kal doubted this bluff soldiering type had any conception of the training a city Archon underwent in the martial, political, and societal arts, if he had he wouldn't be drawing such comparisons.

However, one of the lessons his father and advisers had taught him was that while there was nothing to be gained by speaking it was wisest to remain silent, so he listened attentively to Golconda's story.

'So there we were, me and the rest of my squad, charging around this jungle trying to work out what it could possibly be and annoying the natives no end until we ran into some other world-travellers who were there on some business of their own and they promptly recruited us.'

'And they were from the Wheel?' Kal prompted and Golconda shook his head.

'Not nearly,' he said. 'No, this was before I came to the Wheel. This was a faction who called themselves the Gleaners. We used to bomb through worlds on missions for them, smash-and-grab raids for the most part, although sometimes we found a place we liked and stuck around for a while.' He swung round to look at Kal ominously. 'The fact is the Gleaners weren't the sort of people you'd have liked to meet, lad,' he said. 'Nothing like the Wheel. We weren't much more than glorified bandits and what we gleaned was stuff the locals would have rather kept for themselves.'

'I see,' Kal said, seeing all too much and wondering why the councillor thought this story would endear him to anyone.

'Well, the Gleaners got their come-uppance in the end,' Golconda went on. 'Ran into one of the Wheel's worlds more than twenty years ago and started messing about there. We were pretty pleased with ourselves at first. Nice place, good food, pretty girls, lots of trade goods. No army to speak of.' He made a harrumphing sound of laughter and shook his head at his foolishness. 'Didn't realize that the government was allied to the Wheel, hadn't even heard of such a thing. Were we surprised when they imported an army of crack troops from another one of their worlds and dumped them in through a Door we didn't know about!'

'Crack troops?'

'Oh, definitely.' Golconda nodded vigorously. 'I know because I ended up going through the same training once the Wheel had salvaged me. You see the Wheel doesn't tolerate others messing with them and theirs, and they didn't like the Gleaners at all. Wasn't much left by the time the Wheel finished with us. But a few, like me, got salvaged and now here I am.'

The councillor looked pleased with himself and with an effort Kal smiled back at him, although his mind was racing down unpleasant paths that left him feeling sickened by their conclusion.

'You see, lad,' Golconda went on, resting a friendly arm around his shoulders. 'I was just a regular soldier, didn't know anything about the Library or the Collegiate, but the Wheel took me in and built me up. Now you,' he looked assessingly down at Kal, 'you're young but you ruled this city by yourself, might even have advanced further; there are plenty of opportunities for a lad like you in the Wheel.'

'I'm sure there are, councillor,' Kal agreed, realizing that the time had come to make some sort of commitment. 'But at the moment I'm finding myself a little cramped here. Morgan and I are sharing a room with the twins and well . . .' he smiled slyly, 'it's not exactly conducive to privacy.'

'Aha, I take your point.' Golconda laughed out loud and Kal had to fight to preserve his polite expression. 'Well, as long as we're all on the same side, I think we can find a way to accommodate you.'

'That would help me to adjust, I'm sure,' Kal said, still smiling pleasantly. This was the kind of bargaining a man like Golconda would understand. 'So, what sort of thing do you think I might do for the Wheel in return?'

* * *

Once they'd traversed the Crossway, Zoë found she was beginning to notice the variations and differences between different sections of the Library and the factions that controlled them. Climbing the stairs of the bizarre crossroads she'd seen slices of the Library displayed like a diagram as they climbed upwards past balconies and bookshelves.

One level was plastered with posters and signs giving details of the by-laws of the local faction; the next one up was a hive of activity as people constantly came and went with armloads and boxes of books, trading and swapping them among themselves; another level was all but empty aside from four armed men glowering at them from their guard position in front of the entrance to the section. It was as if the Library was a world of its own and each faction a different country or city inside it.

'You could spend forever just exploring the Library,' Zoë said out loud and Glossali glanced back at her to nod.

'Some people do just that,' he told her. 'But not even the wisest of the Mapmakers knows how far the Library truly extends or at what point in history it originated. Each faction tries to keep record books, of course, but . . . ' He shrugged eloquently. 'The oldest books I've ever seen all referred to others older still.'

'But these Jurists you're taking us to are supposed to be an ancient faction,' Laura said and Glossali hurriedly reassured her.

'Oh yes, the oldest in this part of the Library and they specialize in the history and customs of the Collegiate itself, so I'm certain they'll be able to give you good advice. But it's the faction that's old, you know, not the people who belong to it. They've just come along and joined like anybody else because they got interested in what the Jurists were doing.'

However, it seemed to Zoë that most of the Collegiate members they'd seen so far were old, at least compared to her or the other members of their group. She'd noticed a few young people but the vast majority of those she'd passed were middle-aged or older. Perhaps younger world-travellers didn't spend much time in the Library and went out travelling instead, she mused. All the same it was noticeable enough for her to mention quietly to Jhezra.

'They are mostly men as well,' the Hajhi girl pointed out. 'Perhaps one woman or girl for every ten men, and I've seen no children either.' She frowned. 'I think it's not a true place, this Library. It's not the place where people really live, just somewhere that they visit.' She glanced up at the corridor which had closed in again around them and the ceiling only a few metres above her head. 'And I think I understand why; after so long creeping about these tunnels I wouldn't mind visiting any world, as long as it was out in the air.'

'Does it affect you that badly?' Zoë asked sympathetically, seeing how her friend might feel claustrophobic after growing up in the freedom of the desert.

'Not so much.' Jhezra flashed her a quick smile. 'But I hope we won't have to stay here for too long before seeing the sky again. Have you thought what questions we should ask these Jurists, at all?'

'Well, I want to try and find out if they know a way back to Earth,' Zoë began but Alex interrupted her suddenly, coming up alongside them.

'In that case, you should try and buy a map or something,' he said. 'I'm more interested in getting a handle on who really runs the Collegiate. These Jurists sound like a competent bunch for a change. Perhaps we can do some kind of deal with them.'

'Aren't you a bit worried about the Collegiate rules Glossali's been talking about,' she asked, dropping her voice as she added: 'What happened back in Shattershard could get you in trouble if anyone found out.'

'Nonsense.' Alex glared at her. 'We didn't even know about the Collegiate then. I don't see what that has to do with anything.'

Zoë hesitated but, with Glossali walking only a few paces ahead, she didn't think this was a good time to get into another argument about it and she subsided.

'I would like to know more about the Collegiate too, Alexander,' Jhezra said as the moment of awkwardness passed. 'This Library, for example, someone must have built it. But of what or how I cannot begin to imagine.'

'Come to think of it, something else I'd like to know is how many of these people have magic,' Alex added, looking around him thoughtfully. 'I mean, if they all come from different worlds there could be quite a few of them with magic powers.'

'Maybe someone here will be able to heal Laura,' Zoë agreed.

'Well, yes, that too, of course,' Alex said hastily, his expression making it clear that he'd completely forgotten his sister's blindness. 'But we kind of ignored magic back in Jhezra's world . . . I'd like to know how it's even possible in a scientific universe.'

Jhezra looked blank and Alex waved the comment away, turning his attention to her instead. But Zoë felt troubled. Alex still hadn't accepted responsibility for the collapse of Shattershard and she thought his sudden interest in magic was probably another idea for achieving power and position in a world he could dominate. He didn't seem to have grasped that the Collegiate disapproved of that kind of attitude. Looking ahead at Glossali, leading them into Jurist territory with Laura on his arm, Zoë wondered if this was such a good idea.

When Kal got back to the twins' room Morgan was waiting for him. She was sitting on the small sofa leafing through a book but she turned when she heard him come in and leapt up instantly.

'How was it?' he asked, pushing her hair out of her face so he could look at her properly. 'Was it all right? What happened?'

'It was OK,' Morgan told him, hugging him back tightly. 'But strange. It reminded me of being back at school.'

'Really?' Kal looked thoughtful. 'That doesn't sound so different from my experience. But come and tell me about it.'

As Morgan repeated what she'd told Periphrast and his responses, Kal listened with a growing sense of unease. Being separated from Morgan, even for so short a time, had reminded him how vulnerable they were in the centre of the Wheel's territory. Ciren and Charm might have treated them courteously but he still didn't trust the twins or the Council they so evidently reported to. Now, faced with the certainty that the Wheel was trying to convert him and Morgan to its side, he was alarmed at what that might entail.

Periphrast Diabasis might have convinced Morgan that he could help her control her magic but Kal suspected a more sinister dimension to the secretary's apparent helpfulness.

'What about your orientation?' Morgan's question interrupted his musings. 'How did that go?'

'It was interesting,' Kal said, threading his fingers through Morgan's as he sat back beside her on the sofa. 'The councillor who spoke to me was called Golconda Moraine and he seems to be in charge of an army for the Wheel. However, before that he was a kind of bandit . . .'

He repeated the story about the Gleaners that Golconda had told him and Morgan shivered as he finished.

'They sound frightening,' she said, 'these Gleaners. I don't blame the Wheel for getting rid of them. Why do you think they let this Golconda person join with them?'

'Perhaps they thought he would be useful,' Kal said.

Morgan nodded, looking back at the stack of magic books piled at one end of the sofa, and Kal bit his lips to keep himself from speaking.

For the Wheel to salvage someone as dangerous as Golconda Moraine had told him all too much about the kind of people the faction wanted to recruit. The Wheel coveted power as much as the Tetrarchate and they seemed unscrupulous about getting it.

'Morgan,' he said, touching her shoulder gently, 'what are you going to do about your magic? Do you want to stay here and study with the Wheel?'

'I think I had better,' she told him, her expression troubled. 'There's still so much I don't understand. I told you I wasn't really a powerful mage. We don't even have magic on Earth. But I was wearing black when I first came to Shattershard and people just assumed I was so I thought maybe I'd try doing some magic.' She turned to meet his eyes and smiled weakly. 'I never could do all that much. I could conjure a fire-spark and light a witch-globe and I was happy just to have magic at all. I tried telling the others about it but they weren't interested. I don't think Laura believed my magic was anything more than a party trick. She and Alex were obsessed with politics and influence . . . they used to spend their free time making lists of things they could sell in Shattershard. I think Alex even made up spreadsheets . . .'

Kal frowned, in a moment of incomprehension, and Morgan smiled ruefully, shaking her head in a gesture of dismissal.

'It doesn't matter,' she went on. 'I'd about decided I wanted to live in Shattershard for good when you met me. I thought I'd go on learning magic and maybe someday I'd get good enough to really claim to be a black mage but I never planned to hurt anyone.' She twisted her fingers together and looked down at them unhappily: 'I wanted to hurt Laura. I could have killed her. Everything just burst out of me in this black cloud.' Her voice shook as she added: 'A cloud of hate.'

'Morgan,' Kal reached out to cover her hands with his, stilling them, and he waited until she looked up at him again. 'The first time I killed a man was when I was fifteen. I did patrol duty with the city guard for two years before I had to take the throne. One night a group of thugs rushed three of us, we were outnumbered and they were armed, but we won out because among us we killed two of them.' Kal's face was expressionless as he went on. 'Everything happened so fast I barely remember it. But I do remember looking at the body of one of the men and realizing that I was the one who'd killed him.'

Morgan bit her lip and looked down at their joined hands, trying to find something to say. But Kal hadn't finished:

'There are many kinds of power,' he said quietly. 'To wield a blade, or lead an army, or rule a kingdom and have the power of life and death over your people. But I think that the most awe-inspiring power is magic because it happens at the speed of thought. As you will something, it becomes.'

Morgan's hand tightened around Kal's and she nodded slowly, recognizing the truth of what he said.

'With magic there's no option for second thoughts,' she said. 'You can't take back what you've done.'

9

When Zoë first entered the Jurist section of the Library she was on the lookout for anything that would tell her more about the faction who inhabited it. At first there was nothing obviously different, except that the long corridors were sometimes interrupted by stairs. Sometimes only a couple of steps up round the bend of a corridor, here and there a small flight of stairs with a smooth wooden railing or a tightly coiled spiral winding up around a pillar.

But before long Glossali paused in his route and pointed out an arched doorway a little distance ahead.

'The Hall of Echoes,' he said. 'One of the rooms under the Jurists' especial care . . . Would you like to see it?'

'I won't be able to see it,' Laura pointed out. 'But I don't mind if the others would like to.'

'Why not?' Alex said and Jhezra nodded.

'I'd be interested,' Zoë agreed and Glossali beckoned them onwards.

'It's ancient,' he told them. 'But people still use it. It's a place where Collegiate members can leave messages for each other.'

As the guide led them through the archway Zoë found herself in a cavernous room shaped something like a beehive. The walls were lined with tiny compartments, each just large enough to hold a small scroll of paper, and she could glimpse coloured ribbons and ties fluttering from the edge of some of the compartments. Across the centre of the room stretched two long tables each with a stack of pieces of paper, sticks of coloured sealing wax, and an assortment of pens.

Their footsteps rang softly on the polished floor and a couple of people seated at the tables glanced up as they entered before turning back to their messages. One, a middle-aged woman with greying hair, had several slips of paper stacked up next to her, each of which was neatly folded and sealed with a wax impression like letters waiting for the post. At her feet a reddish-coated dog lay patiently waiting for her to finish and as Zoë and her companions entered it raised its head to look at them before yawning and resting its snout between its front paws again.

'There's no real system for finding messages,' Glossali whispered. 'So visitors have to search all the compartments for a ribbon or a seal they recognize. As the compartments get full the Jurists remove the older messages, but I don't know what happens to them then.'

'They go into the vaults.' The woman with the dog addressed her last message and folded it swiftly as she spoke to them. 'There they are shelved by year rather than having compartments to themselves. But no message is ever discarded.'

'Well, there you see then,' Glossali said, looking a bit surprised and Jhezra made a gesture of thanks. The woman smiled back at her and walked up to the rows of compartments and while Glossali continued his whispered explanations to Laura, Zoë watched with interest as the stranger began posting her messages.

She had begun where there was a line of six empty compartments and she filled each of them seemingly at random from her stack of folded messages, before glancing about and putting another four or five into other compartments nearby. Then she deliberately crossed the room and seemed to be searching for particular places to put the last three, her dog padding patiently behind her.

'Could I write a message, do you think?' Zoë asked and Glossali turned to look at her.

'I don't see why not,' he said.

'Who would you write to?' Laura asked, as Zoë went and took a piece of paper and a pen. Her voice went suddenly suspicious as she added: 'Morgan?'

'No,' Zoë said simply. 'To my dad.'

'Why?' Alex looked completely bemused as he turned to stare at her. 'Your dad doesn't even know about world-travelling. Why write to him?'

'Because if he ever came to this place he'd look for a message from me,' Zoë replied shortly.

She didn't take long, not wanting to delay the others; besides the words came easily when she thought about them. There wasn't much to say except that she was sorry and she hoped they'd see each other again. But in a weird way writing it actually made her feel worse, as if her dad was dead and she was writing a card to send with flowers. When she looked up again from her completed message, Jhezra's eyes were sympathetic.

'What will you use to identify yourself?' she asked and Zoë hesitated, glancing down at her jacket.

'One of these straps,' she said indicating a strip of leather buckled round her sleeve. 'My dad gave me this coat,' she explained, freeing the strap she wanted. 'Can you cut it for me, Jhezra?'

'Of course,' her friend said, unsheathing her dagger and neatly slicing off the piece she wanted. 'Perhaps you should leave a lock of your hair as well, just to be sure?'

'OK,' Zoë agreed and held still while Jhezra carefully lifted up the mass of her hair and teased one strand away from the rest.

'There,' she said, cutting it with one swift motion of her knife and handing it to Zoë. 'Now he will be certain to know which message is yours.'

Solemnly Zoë climbed a set of Library steps and tucked her scroll of paper in one of the empty alcoves while Jhezra watched. Laura and Glossali waited patiently and Alex peered into the nearby compartments while she left the message.

'Perhaps some day your father will come into the Library,' Jhezra said softly. 'Or maybe you'll find a way home and see him again.'

'Maybe,' Zoë said, as she rejoined the others on the floor. 'But even if I can I won't be the same person who left. I'll have been gone for too long. How can I ever explain what's happened to me since then?'

Jhezra bowed her head in admission that what she said was true and Zoë swallowed because she couldn't speak. But as she blinked away tears, across the expanse of the room she saw that the middle-aged woman had finished placing her own messages and stood watching them, her eyes narrowed with curious interest.

Charm was finding it hard to concentrate on the book she was reading. She was used to sharing a room, or a tent, or even a bed with her twin, but it wasn't as easy to share space with Morgan and Kal.

Sitting at the table, she bent over her book and tried to block out the soft conversation coming from the other side of the room. Periphrast Diabasis had provided Morgan with a large pile of elementary magic textbooks and some more esoteric works on magical theory from various worlds. With little else to do Kal was helping her read through the theory works, bringing interesting points to her notice, while Ciren stayed nearby to answer some of her general questions.

'Each world possesses a unique magical field,' Kal was reading out from one of the books. 'It is from this that practising mages in the locality draw their power and it is replenished by the release of those powers back into the world. The power of all magical effects may increase or decrease dependent on the strength of the surrounding magical field. The exception to this is the Library which is surmised to maintain a magical field at the level of the universal average.'

'I don't think I understood one word in three of that,' Morgan admitted and Ciren laughed.

Caging her head in her hands Charm tried to block out their conversation, staring down at a paragraph she'd already read twice before. The book was the one by Caravaggion of Mandarel that Ciren had lent her the night before and its title was *The Doors of Mandarel.* Last night she'd found it so fascinating it was with reluctance that she'd finally put it away but today it just didn't seem to be holding her attention.

Glancing back at the three clustered around the sofa Charm wondered how long she and Ciren would have to be responsible for Morgan and Kal. They'd never worked closely with other agents for long; Vespertine's assignments had kept them moving from world to world. Already she was feeling tired of being cooped up in a room with two random natives and it didn't help that Ciren seemed almost relieved not to be alone with her.

Resting her chin on her hands Charm continued to watch the others and slowly, deliberately, her mouth formed a cold smile. Her mind reached out across the room, skirting carefully past Ciren's mind with its tantalizing psyche twinned to her own. Next to him Kal's mind fluttered like a moth trapped inside a glass jar; it was there but unreachable. But Morgan's mind was open and defenceless and Charm received her loud and clear; everything from her scattered surface musings to her innermost secret intents.

Charm sifted through the confusion trying to discover what Morgan thought of the Wheel; there was just so much she didn't understand in the Earth girl's mind, huge swatches of memories and influences that meant nothing to her, she could take years to assimilate it. There were wonders and marvels inside Morgan's memories but Charm couldn't find the answer to her question. Morgan seemed to be still working out what she thought about the Wheel, and her impression of Kal was that he was also still making up his mind. Nothing conclusive, Charm thought irritably as she withdrew and returned her concentrating to her own body just in time to see a pair of wide green eyes staring at her with sudden alarm.

'Did you just read my mind again?' Morgan demanded and Kal and Ciren swung round to stare at Charm as well.

'I'm surprised you noticed,' Charm said. 'You haven't the last couple of times.'

'I thought you promised you weren't going to do it at all . . . ' Morgan said angrily and Charm shrugged.

'Ciren told you that,' she said. 'And in any case the circumstances have changed. The Council considers us responsible for you. That means I need to know what you're thinking.'

'I disagree,' Kal said abruptly and his gaze shifted back to Ciren. 'I'm unconvinced by that argument. If we're guests here, why should we be treated like prisoners?' Then he stopped speaking as suddenly as he'd begun, folding his lips over words as yet unsaid.

Charm stared at him, her face set hard as she tried to work out what Kal really thought. But with his mind blocked to her, she had no way of guessing. Ciren, meanwhile, looked troubled and his gaze shifted from Morgan and Kal's indignant expressions to look back at Charm.

'Is it really necessary . . . ' he began and Charm felt a stab of pain at the betrayal.

'Of course it's necessary,' she insisted, standing up and pushing her chair back with a sharp gesture. 'You know what our patron expects of us . . . ' She could feel her face tightening angrily as she confronted her twin. 'We're responsible for them,' she flicked a hand at Kal and Morgan, 'you know what that means . . . '

Ciren's face tightened in annoyance and he opened his mouth to speak and Charm suddenly decided she didn't want to hear it. Standing beside Morgan and Kal her twin seemed immeasurably distant from her. Ever since those two had joined them he'd been making difficulties when the path ahead seemed clear and causing confusion over questions when they had no choice.

'No,' she said. 'No more. Suffice to say that we disagree.' Her eyes met Ciren's and saw her own hurt and confusion reflected back from their purple depths and she looked away and past him as she walked out of the room.

Zoë had seemed to need some time to recover herself after their visit to the Hall of Echoes and Jhezra, walking beside her, occupied herself in looking around.

The Jurist section of the Library seemed more friendly than others they had passed by. The corridors were well lit and, in addition to the predictable book-lined shelves, there were a number of obvious innovations. There were signs everywhere and notices on single sheets of paper tacked to the shelf sections which she caught glimpses of as they walked by. *'Have removed Tishlin's Thesis on the Worlds of Light Mythos for further study.—Sojourner Haruspex'*; *'Biographies of the World-Travellers, discussion group meets peripatetically in the rooms of Oscura Umbra'*; and *'Open Debate—Wine and Savouries Provided—Visitors Welcome'* outside a room where a couple of people had smiled and beckoned when she'd glanced through the archway.

Jhezra considered accepting the clear invitation, but Glossali was still obviously leading the way some distance ahead and she'd had to content herself with a brief bow to the friendly faces. However, it seemed that the Jurists were generally welcoming. The people they saw in the corridor would nod or murmur some polite greeting as they passed and Jhezra found herself returning them the same courtesy.

Jhezra wondered if Zoë was intending to travel through the whole Library looking for a path back to Earth or the world of the Tetrarchate. It was beginning to seem as if such an endeavour could last the rest of their lives and perhaps it might be worthwhile putting down roots somewhere near a place like this where the people were friendly and there was so much to learn. In the area of the Catalogue Cultists she'd felt daunted by the quantity of books and how irrelevant they seemed to anything she knew about life. But this faction was more intriguing and perhaps one of the Doors they passed might lead into a world which would make her welcome.

When Glossali Intergrade finally halted it came as something of a surprise and Jhezra had to tap Zoë's arm lightly to get her attention. Laura and Alex had stopped as well and stood waiting for them a little way ahead. The corridor here was wide and on either side little flights of stairs led up to a series of rooms, each one with a sign outside presumably bearing the name of the occupant.

'Well, this is the Jurist section and I think I'll leave you here,' Glossali told them. 'I'm heading on to the Converse Court,' he explained, pointing down the corridor to where a staircase dropped steeply downwards. 'Don't worry, it's just down there and if you get lost anyone in this section can tell you the way. But if you're looking for advice the people in these rooms can probably help you better than I can.'

'Oh.' Zoë seemed to have recovered herself as she said politely, 'It was very kind of you to bring us this far.'

'I'm sure we'll see you again,' Laura added. 'We'll be able to find you in the Converse Court?'

'For at least the next couple of days,' Glossali confirmed. Putting down his sack of belongings, he took Laura's hands affectionately. 'Good luck to you,' he said warmly. 'I hope you can find what you're looking for.'

'Thanks for your help,' Alex said, as Glossali turned to him and Jhezra stepped forward.

'I'm sorry for the misunderstanding when we first met,' she said, remembering how she'd captured the cringing Catalogue Cultist.

'Oh well.' Glossali shrugged a shoulder. 'No hard feelings. I hope we'll meet up again sometime.' His eyes strayed one last smile to Laura before he picked up his sack again and set off down the corridor, turning to wave at them before setting his feet on the first step of the steep stairway.

'Goodbye!' Zoë called after him.

As the young Catalogue Cultist disappeared from sight Jhezra found herself feeling interested. Now that she had her translation charm she didn't feel as daunted by the idea of meeting new faction members and she was curious to discover what these Jurists were like.

'Well,' said Alex, turning to look at the line of arched entrances to the rooms. 'Which one should we pick?'

When Charm left her room it was with no clear idea of where she was headed and she realized almost immediately that she felt uncomfortable without her two short swords. But the abiding influence that had forced her out of the room was still directing her away from Ciren and the others and she walked around and around the familiar corridors she had grown up in, not noticing what route she took. It was a surprise to find herself in front of the entrance to the Chamber of the Wheel.

The room was empty and she walked inside with a sense of awe. Although entry wasn't strictly speaking proscribed, it was one of the many things that it was necessary to be careful about in the Wheel, and she'd never been in this room except to report to members of the faction's Council.

Circling around the great table she looked with interest at the books on the walls. Although this was the centre of the Wheel's power the books kept here weren't considered to be of very great value since most Wheel members hid their most important books in their rooms or in private caches on worlds they controlled. All the same, the books here did hold the Wheel's personal records since the faction's creation and, on an impulse, Charm searched the shelves for the records for eight years ago.

It was a thick volume, bound in red and black leather, with glyphs on the spine which were used only for Wheel records. Charm could read them with the powers of her obsidian amulet but they were arranged in an order designed to baffle lesser magics. Flipping slowly through the pages she came at last to the entry she was looking for:

'Proceedings of the Council: Vespertine Chalcedony announced his acquisition of a new asset, two juvenile mages he acquired through sources on his home world. The children will be initiated into the Wheel under his auspices.'

Charm read further down the page but there was nothing more and she shut the book and returned it to its position on the shelf. Vespertine had never told her or Ciren anything more about where they came from. They had been brought up knowing only that they belonged to him and must serve the Wheel and that it was an honour to do so. Up until now she'd never considered questioning that. She'd enjoyed their training in the Collegiate, visiting different worlds and reading the minds and magic of the people. She'd been amused by the way they'd so often been dismissed as children by people whose secrets they learnt and then delivered to their patron. The Wheel's worlds were pleasant and profited under their effective organization but some still contained rebels who resisted the Wheel's influence and while there were new frontiers to be conquered there would always be rebels. Charm had read the minds of many of them and Ciren had read their magical defences and armed with that knowledge the Wheel had conquered.

Vespertine had also taken them to worlds controlled by the Wheel where they'd been treated like princes and told them that when they were older they could have their own establishments anywhere the Wheel held sway. It was an enticing vision of the future and the twins had succeeded beyond anyone's expectation as agents of the Wheel. They worked so well as a unit that Vespertine had never separated them. In the past few years he had permitted them to travel alone and up until now they'd been perfectly content. But now Ciren had called into question everything they knew about themselves and Charm was left wondering what that meant for their future.

They hadn't chosen this life and yet she'd never thought to question it. But under the influence of Morgan and Kal, it seemed Ciren was doing exactly that and Charm feared . . . She hardly knew what she feared, although she was certain that they could never leave the Wheel or go against their patron's commands. But she also couldn't bear to be parted from her twin. Ciren was her second self, the other half of her mind, and she couldn't imagine existing without him.

Charm turned away from the red and black wheel and left the chamber. Her head was full of voices asking questions she couldn't begin to answer by herself. It wasn't possible for her to live so divided from her twin; they would have to talk again and this time she was determined to discover all the doubts Ciren had been keeping from her.

Zoë glanced up and down the corridor, feeling somewhat daunted. But as her gaze caught a sign posted outside one of the rooms she realized what their next step should be. The sign she was looking at read: *'Persiflage Demosthene: Scholar and Jurist: Experienced Accountant and Financier'*.

Moving automatically along to read the next sign, Zoë caught the others' attention.

'Look at the signs next to the rooms, you guys,' she said. 'We should find one of these that seems to help. Maybe something about maps or something like tourist advice.'

Jhezra obediently followed after her, checking the signs on the other side of the corridor as they retraced their recent path along it. Alex started moving in the opposite direction, reading out the signs he saw to Laura as he came to them.

'This looks useful,' he called down to them after a minute. 'Tan Ecesis, it says he's a magician and healer.' But when he knocked at the entrance there was no reply.

'Maybe he's out having lunch or something,' Zoë said, looking back at Laura. 'We can try again later perhaps?'

'Or ask one of his neighbours if they know where he is,' Laura pointed out, seemingly quite calm.

Jhezra had continued on down the corridor and Zoë followed after her, as Laura and Alex continued in the other direction.

'Sibalent Askew, Peregrinade Poet,' she read out loud. 'Germane Redoubt, Jurist Philosopher, open if light is green.' She glanced up to see a lantern hanging above the arched entrance to the room but the shade was an amber gold and she moved on quickly in case she'd disturbed anyone inside the room.

'Lisle Weft of Fenrisnacht, Jurist,' Jhezra turned to say, reading from the next sign as Zoë caught up. 'Messages can be left here for Caravaggion of Mandarel.'

Zoë nodded vaguely and had moved on to the next entrance when a sudden memory made her swing back and exclaim:

'What was that?'

'Lisle Weft,' Jhezra repeated, looking surprised. 'And this extra sign next to it.'

'Caravaggion of Mandarel,' Zoë read out loud, coming to look. 'It does say that . . . ' She stared at the innocuous piece of paper pinned next to the room's entrance, remembering the warmth of Dynan's forge and the words of advice he'd left her with: *'The wisest man I met was someone called Caravaggion of Mandarel. It was he who taught me the folly of ever giving advice.'*

'Zoë?' Jhezra looked concerned. 'What is it?'

'Caravaggion,' Zoë repeated, still dumbfounded. 'I know that name.'

'Is that so?'

Zoë blinked and Jhezra spun on her heel, one hand flying to the hilt of her scimitar, as they realized that someone had come up behind them. It was the elderly woman Zoë had seen in the Hall of Echoes and beside her the red dog raised its hackles and growled ominously deep in its throat.

'You surprised us,' Zoë said, tapping Jhezra's arm quickly to make her drop her hand from the sword hilt.

'Really? Since you're standing outside my study I assumed you were waiting for me,' the woman said drily, with a gesture that made the dog calm down again. 'My name is Lisle Weft. How can I help you?'

When Charm stormed out of the room, Morgan and Kal had exchanged looks but said nothing. Ciren, staring down at the heap of magic books, still seemed stunned by his twin's sudden anger. Kal looked uncomfortable in the aftermath of the argument and picked up his own book, pretending to read it.

Morgan didn't know what to do. She was still angry and scared about Charm's deliberate reading of her mind and confused by the way Ciren seemed to have been defending them. That cryptic comment about 'responsibility' had worried her as well and she wondered yet again what exactly the Wheel expected of them. It was almost a relief when Ciren stood up suddenly with an abrupt movement in contrast to his usual calm.

'I have to go,' he said. 'I have to find Charm. Excuse me.'

He didn't wait for them to reply, heading for the exit,

and as he left the room Morgan could hear the pace of his steps increasing so that he was almost running by the time the sound faded out of hearing.

'Well,' she said, looking at Kal. 'That was strange.'

'No, it wasn't,' he said seriously and she was surprised to see an oddly determined look on his face as he met her eyes. 'Morgan,' he said. 'We need to talk.'

Morgan shivered. In her experience the phrase 'we need to talk' never led to anything good. For a moment she even wondered if Kal was about to break up with her but from his first words she realized that his concerns were of a far greater order.

'I don't trust the Wheel,' he told her. She gasped in sudden surprise and he gripped her hand as he continued quickly. 'I don't trust Ciren and Charm and I don't trust the Council or that Vespertine Chalcedony who seems to be in charge. I haven't told you before because anything I tell you, Charm can read from your mind.'

'But you've told me now!' Morgan exclaimed in alarm and Kal nodded.

'Yes, and we might not have much time, so you're going to have to decide quickly what you want to do.'

'What?' She bit her lips, feeling confused by the sudden pressure and clung to his hand as if it was a lifeline. 'What do you mean, decide?'

'Morgan,' Kal's voice was deeply serious, 'the Wheel wants to use you for your magic and they want to use me in their wars. They're not peaceful or benevolent. They've got a foothold on my world now and I'm fairly certain they're involved with the Tetrarchate government. I'm not sure how much we can trust what they've told us about the Collegiate but if it's true they've been breaking half the Collegiate's rules and bending the others . . . ' He took a deep breath and then added: 'And as soon as Charm discovers what I've told you she'll report me to her patron.

Maybe Ciren wouldn't but I can't rely on that. I have to get out of here. Now.'

Already he was backing off from her and finding his travel pack from the chest where he'd stored it, throwing in clothes and food haphazardly and dumping a couple of books in the top before buckling it up tightly. Watching him in shock, Morgan couldn't believe what was happening.

'You're leaving me?' she tried to ask and it came out as a thin whisper.

'God, Morgan, no!' Kal's grey eyes were pleading. 'I don't want to. But I can't stay here . . . and we don't have any time . . . Will you come with me?'

'Of course I will,' she stammered, overcome with relief. 'I don't care about the Wheel. I don't ca . . . care about anything except you.'

'Oh, Morgan.' One hand strapping on his sword, Kal pulled her close with the other but he released her again almost as quickly. 'Hurry, then, grab your things, and those books too. You might need them.'

'Shouldn't we at least write some kind of note though?' Morgan asked as she tumbled her few possessions into her own bag. 'To let the twins know why we left?'

'I think they'll know all too well,' Kal said grimly, hoisting his pack on his back. 'Come now. We've no time to lose.'

Ciren hardly knew what direction he was walking in as he searched for his twin through the territory of the Wheel. When he eventually saw her approaching from the other end of a long corridor he felt a rush of sheer relief and ran to meet her, reaching out to clasp her hands with his.

'Forgive me,' he said. 'I don't know what I was thinking. How could you just leave like that?'

Charm's black-purple eyes met his as if from some immeasurable distance away and she shook her head.

'I don't know,' she said wonderingly. 'I just had to. But my mind doesn't seem to work properly when we're apart . . . or when we disagree. Ciren, we have to solve this.'

'I know.' He bent his head in agreement before looking back at her. 'But how?'

'You know how.' Charm stared back at him. 'Let me read your mind, then I'll know what's really troubling you. Then we'll be able to agree again.'

'Are you sure that we'll agree?' Ciren asked. 'If even I don't know what's at the root of my uncertainty, how can you be sure you'll be able to discover it in my mind, or that if you do we'll be able to dispel it.'

'Do you have another option?' Charm asked and, as he hesitated, she smiled.

He had to fight the urge to say no, to back off or run away. Charm had never read his mind before, he'd always believed their partnership was so close that she would never need to. But Charm had never been apart from him before either, not for as far back as he could remember.

As she smiled Ciren's magical sense reached out, tasting the texture of a magic similar to his and yet curiously different. Her black-purple eyes seemed to expand as she stared at him and he felt her mind reaching out to touch his. Ciren couldn't know what it was her other victims felt, in fact most of them seemed not even to notice the invasion of their minds, but his own powers allowed him to sense Charm's. He could feel the otherness touching his thoughts and it was all he could do not to recoil from that terrible invasive exploration.

'It's done,' she said, and he felt her magic retreating. 'I've gone as deep as I dare.' A frown ran across her face.

'There are levels I can't reach. You're blocked from me there.'

'I am?' Ciren frowned back at her. 'I wasn't trying to hide anything.'

'You couldn't,' she said simply. 'This is more like memory loss, things you don't remember, maybe from when you were a child.'

'I don't remember much about our childhood,' Ciren realized but Charm dismissed the train of thought.

'It's not important, anyway,' she said. 'I found out what I wanted to know.'

'And?'

Charm's mouth twisted in a grimace of frustration and he could see the answer hadn't pleased her.

'You're conflicted,' she said. 'I don't know why but you are. One part of you feels protective of Kal and Morgan. You don't trust them, on that we're agreed although I hadn't realized how far your doubts went. You seem practically certain they won't join the Wheel. But you hide that certainty from yourself.' She shook her head. 'Your mind . . . it's like someone playing hide and seek with themselves, no wonder you don't know what you think.'

'It is?' Ciren was still trying to assimilate her explanation.

'But there's one thing you know as well as I do,' she said. 'We have to be loyal. We have to do what Vespertine would want. And if you don't trust Morgan and Kal to join us . . .'

'Then we'll have to tell Vespertine.'

10

Lisle Weft's study was the most comfortable room Zoë had seen in the Library. When the Jurist woman had invited them inside she'd accepted willingly, calling Laura and Alex back down the corridor to join them. But it wasn't until Lisle had offered them seats and set a pot of water to boil on an iron brazier that Zoë noticed the really strange thing about the room. It wasn't covered with bookshelves.

There were some shelves. Over in one corner near a desk overloaded with papers were four neat runs of books. But that was it. All over the rest of the room the wooden walls were bare and Zoë could see marks in the otherwise smooth surface where the shelves had been removed.

'Don't you like books?' she found herself asking and then felt embarrassed as the woman laughed at her confusion.

'I like them well enough,' Lisle told her. 'But I don't see any reason to worship them, or to paper my walls with them. But if it's books you're after there are plenty just outside.' She gestured back through the beaded curtain that screened the entrance to the corridor they had just come from.

'You'll have to excuse my young friend,' Alex said with a patronizing air.

'She doesn't need to be apologized for,' Lisle sent Zoë a narrow smile. 'Some people start hoarding books like an animal storing food for the winter, others want to possess them in ever greater numbers or collect them for the attractiveness of their bindings.' She gestured casually to her remaining shelves. 'Personally, I keep a few for reference, and that's it.'

Zoë nodded. She had liked the look of Lisle almost immediately and she felt comfortable in this warm room with its battered chairs and smell of ginger and green tea.

'So, what is it I can do for you?' Lisle asked again and this time Laura was the one to speak.

'We're newcomers to the Library,' she said smoothly. 'And also new to the concept of the Collegiate. Our travels through the worlds brought us here by accident and a chance-met acquaintance advised us that the Jurists were people who might be able to answer our questions and guided us here.'

'I see.' Lisle's expression was thoughtful and one of her large knobbly hands reached out to feel the teapot for warmth before she leant back in her seat. 'Please do go on.'

'We now know a little more about the laws and customs here,' Laura said. 'But we're ignorant of how they might affect us and, without knowing the route to our own worlds, in need of guidance.' She paused for a moment and then sighed audibly, one of her hands lifting to the scarf she had tied once more across her blinded eyes. 'We've also been victims of violence and devastation

. . . as you can see, I'm blind, in consequence of a magical attack.'

'Indeed.' Lisle regarded Laura for a long moment before saying: 'I'm afraid magic isn't a skill I possess but I may know someone who can help you. For now, tell me more about these other problems you mentioned . . . ' She glanced around at them, considering Jhezra with additional curiosity. 'You said none of you know the route back to your home worlds. Is that what you desire, to return?'

'Yes,' said Zoë just as Alex said:

'No.'

'It is complicated,' Jhezra told Lisle, speaking with great politeness. 'I personally would wish return home to be a possibility, even though I am curious to learn more of the other worlds and of your Library.'

'Well, that's an honest answer, at least,' Lisle said drily. 'I hope, since you're carrying weapons, this helpful guide mentioned the restrictions on their use.'

'I know world-travellers are not supposed to harm each other,' Jhezra said carefully. 'I don't yet understand how these rules would apply if I were attacked by another traveller or if I harmed someone in ignorance of their identity.'

'Another honest answer.' Lisle laughed in what sounded like surprise, and got up from her chair to pour boiling water from the pot into five cups, adding a pinch of dried herbs to each one. 'The rule would be applied differently depending on how and where your act was committed.' She handed out the cups carefully to each of them, giving Zoë one to pass on to Laura before giving her one for herself. 'Here in the Jurist section you would be tried in the Converse Court. I think we'd be tolerant in the first instance but suspicious in the second.'

Zoë tried to work that out in her head as she gave Laura

her cup of drink, making sure the other girl had a firm grip on it, and accepted her own. It was a strange flavour of herbal tea but she thought she could get to like it.

'I want to know more about the Collegiate,' Alex was saying. 'Who runs it, how did it start, who decides all these rules?'

'Those are questions many people would like to know the answers to,' Lisle said casually. 'My friend Caravaggion has made it his life's work to discover the secrets of the Library's origins and he's no closer than he was when he first set out on his quest.'

'Caravaggion,' Zoë said softly and Lisle turned to her.

'Yes,' she said. 'It was the notice concerning him that attracted your attention, wasn't it? What is your interest in my friend?'

'Well, someone once gave me some advice,' Zoë said, conscious of the sharp look Alex had turned on her and the listening tilt of Laura's head. 'But it wasn't very good advice. And then he said that the person who'd taught him the folly of giving advice was your friend.'

'Well, it certainly sounds like one of Caravaggion's ideas,' Lisle agreed. 'It has just the right air of seeming to be useful while in fact telling you nothing at all.' She laughed again at Zoë's expression and continued: 'I can see what he means, I think. Giving advice can be dangerous, it serves to indoctrinate another person with your opinions, and if those opinions are wrong . . .' She shook her head. 'But then again, if the advice is to tell you that the water in your well is poisoned or that the path you are following leads to the edge of a cliff, holding back for some philosophical reason seems absurd.'

'Then you're not a philosopher yourself?' Zoë asked shyly and Lisle smiled.

'All old women are philosophers,' she said wryly. 'But no. Nowadays I'm a Jurist, and before that I was a soldier and before that . . . ' A shadow passed across her face. 'Before that I was nothing to speak of.'

As they walked swiftly towards Vespertine's private quarters in the Wheel section the twins saw evidence of some commotion: guard duties seemed to have increased and messengers brushed past them more than once. But the third messenger spun on his heel and came back to them.

'Agents Ciren and Charm?' he demanded and when they identified themselves he frowned importantly. 'There's an alert out for you. Something about students missing from orientation.'

'Kal and Morgan,' Ciren said instantly. 'Where are they?'

'You don't know?' The messenger looked suspicious. 'There's an alert out for them as well seeing that they're not where they're supposed to be.'

'We must speak to Vespertine,' Charm said, stepping past the messenger. 'We haven't got time for this.'

Ciren made haste to follow her and the messenger had to flatten himself against the wall to get out of his way. But the route to Vespertine's rooms was full of guards and they had to show their identifiers more than once to agents who didn't know them. The delay made Charm agitated but Ciren felt detached from himself as he forged his way through the guards. When they finally reached Vespertine's study he didn't pause for a second before stepping inside.

Once there though he froze in place and Charm came to an abrupt halt next to him. Vespertine was sitting alone in a chair, reading a book by the glow of a floating witch-globe, the rest of the room cast into shadow. He looked up, his face wearing the same expression of distant benevolence he had always shown to them.

'Well, my children,' he said. 'It seems you have lapsed in your responsibility.'

'Forgive us, patron, we were wrong,' Charm said and Vespertine turned to look at Ciren, whitened eyes gazing limpidly into his.

'My mind was confused,' he found himself saying stupidly. 'Charm and I didn't agree. But now we are agreed that Morgan and Kal will never join the Wheel. We were coming to tell you when . . .'

'There has been considerable miscommunication,' Vespertine said gently and Ciren wondered why he felt so apprehensive before his patron. 'But both Periphrast Diabasis and Golconda Moraine reported that your young protégés were being reasonable. I would like to discuss this lapse further but time is of the essence . . .'

Vespertine's face was shadowed by the position of the witch-light as he leant forward but Ciren could feel his presence filling the room. His patron's dry papery voice came forth in slow deliberate phrases.

'Morgan and Kal must be retrieved. I have a use for her magic and I want to obtain more information about the item he wears. Therefore you must follow them, find them, and take whatever steps you must to bring them back.'

'Yes, Vespertine.' Charm's obedience was instant and Ciren heard his own voice echoing hers.

'Yes, Vespertine.'

'But don't bring them back here. It was obviously unwise to allow them so much freedom,' Vespertine continued. 'It was a courtesy that will not be extended again. When you find them, bring them to my estate. From now on I will handle this matter in person.'

The twins bowed in unison and Vespertine's withered lips moved in something like a smile.

'Go now, my children. Reaffirm my faith in you.'

'Yes, Vespertine,' they said together and left the room.

Escaping from the Wheel section had been both more difficult and much easier than Kal had anticipated. Before leaving the twins' room he had rummaged through the drawers for a couple of enamelled badges each bearing the red and black symbol of the Wheel. Warning Morgan to look confident, he had pinned one to her clothes and one to his own and set off at a brisk walk through the corridors.

To his surprise the plan worked. The section might be full of Wheel agents but the guards were checking on people who wanted to get closer into the section rather than people heading out. Morgan looked apprehensive, her green eyes large in her pale face, but Kal kept a firm grip on her arm and perhaps the guards they passed assumed he was escorting her somewhere because they didn't question him.

The problem was that the Wheel section was much larger than he'd realized. He'd been hoping that after a while they'd break out of it and into an area of the Library controlled by another more trustworthy faction, or at least one that the Wheel wouldn't want to follow them into. But the curved corridors and scattered stairways were confusing. Kal wasn't even sure of the way back to the Tetrarchate Door. All he could do was keep moving, keep angling away from the centre of Wheel influence and keep hoping that escape was possible.

One of the options he'd forced himself to consider was escaping through a Door but he worried that any world reached from the Wheel territory would be more or less under their influence. Perhaps he and Morgan could hide in such a world but he didn't want to try it as anything other than a last resort. Instead he hoped that what

Periphrast had told Morgan about Collegiate members being forbidden to harm each other was true.

They'd been travelling for nearly two hours when they came across a group of armed Wheel agents standing in guard positions halfway down an otherwise unexceptional corridor. There was no hope they hadn't been noticed; all four Wheel agents turned to look at them as Kal and Morgan came round a branch of the corridor, and Kal decided to put a brave face on it.

'Greetings,' he said politely, squeezing Morgan's hand reassuringly. 'I wonder if you could help us.'

'If it lies within our ability,' one of the agents said with the same stilted politeness he'd often noticed in the twins. 'What would you ask us?'

'We're travelling on business for our patron,' Kal said, trying to remember as much as he could about the political hierarchy of the Wheel. 'But I fear we may have taken a wrong turn. It's taking us longer to leave the Wheel area than we anticipated.'

'You came down the north-west corridor branch?' the agent asked, seeming to accept Kal's explanation. 'You were probably aiming for the Bridge across Darkness then.'

Kal hesitated only momentarily. That was the kind of question that could easily be a trick but the manner of the stranger appeared genuine and he decided to risk it.

'That's right,' he said, putting on an expression of relief. 'But we seem to be going in circles.'

'You certainly are,' the Wheel agent said with a superior smile. 'You should have turned left at guard-post seventeen. It'll take you nearly an hour to get back on track now.'

'An hour!' Morgan exclaimed, joining in the conversation with a convincing air of distress. 'But our patron told us the message was urgent. He'll be furious if he finds out we've been so careless.'

The Wheel agent actually looked sympathetic at Morgan's obvious alarm and he frowned in thought for a moment before suddenly taking a sheaf of folded paper from his tunic.

'Well, you may be able to retrieve your mistake,' he said. 'Look, this is where you are now. Guard-post twenty-three. See?' He shuffled through the papers and directed their attention to a neatly drawn map as the other guards drew closer with interested expressions.

Kal scanned the map as quickly as he could. The Wheel agent had to bring out a couple more pages to show them the correspondence to levels of the Library above and below where they were now. The Wheel section was marked out clearly in thick black lines with smaller spidery script in a variety of different handwritings listing names of corridors, positions of guard-posts, and worlds reached through Doors. Where the agent pointed the number 23 was plainly written and a few of the nearby regions were labelled in capital letters: Engravers, Cryptographers, Jurists.

As they puzzled over the maps the Wheel agents seemed to take a friendly interest in their problem.

'As our influence expands navigating the section is increasingly difficult,' the leader of the group told them. 'Even agents who've been with the Wheel for years can be caught out by unexpected twists in the corridors. Now where did you say you were bound?'

'Oh,' Kal's eyes travelled quickly to where the number seventeen was marked on the map and then beyond it, 'to the Cryptographer section.'

'Ah, well in that case you can probably make up most of your time by skirting the edge of this section here,' the agent said, showing them a route on the map that twisted past the block letters reading 'Jurists'.

'Yes, I see,' Kal said, studying the map carefully. 'Up

these stairs and then a left . . . ' He recited directions for a while longer before adding casually, 'Do you know anything about these Jurists?'

'Not much,' the agent said with a grimace. 'We've only recently been assigned here. But they seem to be a legally minded group by the name.'

'Thank you for your help anyway,' Morgan said as the agent rolled up the map. 'You've saved us from being any further delayed.'

'And good luck to you on your mission,' the agent replied. 'Perhaps we'll meet again on your way back.'

'Perhaps,' Kal said, noncommittally. 'But we may take a better route next time.'

As they followed the corridor to where a staircase suddenly climbed sharply upwards he felt the gazes of the guards watching them and it wasn't until they were out of sight that he felt able to take a deep breath of relief.

'That was lucky,' Morgan breathed softly. 'You were wonderful, Kal.'

'You weren't bad yourself,' he smiled at her. 'But we're not out of the woods yet.'

The magician they found for Laura spent more than two hours studying her eyes. Alex fidgeted uncomfortably in a straight-backed chair in the man's office wondering why he had to be the one to wait with her. It wasn't as if Laura especially needed him there; she sat patiently being examined and asking the mage occasional questions and refusing all offers of food or drink.

Lisle Weft had led them all to the magician's study before offering to show Zoë and Jhezra around the Jurist section some more. Alex had hinted that Laura didn't really need his company but it hadn't got him anywhere and instead he'd been forced to agree that they'd meet up with the others later at the place Glossali Intergrade had mentioned. According to Lisle this Converse Court was an important room for the Jurist section and a common place for people to agree to meet. Alex wished he was there now. There might be important people there or even someone who could sell him a sword or at the very least offer him a drink. But instead he had nothing to do but sit and moulder while he waited for Laura.

There were books on a side table but they all seemed to be pages of meditation exercises. Alex had tried a couple of them, closing his eyes and imagining a flame or concentrating on his own heartbeat. But it was too easy to get bored and he put the books back again.

'Reluctantly, I'm going to have to admit that this is beyond my power to cure,' someone said and Alex sat up in his chair. The magician's name was one of the jumbles of syllables Alex had come to expect in the Library and it took him a few seconds to remember what it had been. 'I'm very sorry, Laura Harrell.'

Alex remembered eventually that the mage had been introduced as Tan Ecesis and raised his hand to attract the man's attention but Laura was already speaking.

'But when we got here you seemed certain you knew what was wrong with my vision,' she objected and Tan Ecesis looked despondent.

'I am certain,' the mage explained. 'You have been cursed. The spell is not directed specifically at your eyes or your vision. It is a magical effect that works on your essence of self. It therefore cannot be counteracted by another spell. The curse will remain until it is removed.'

'Then I'll be blind forever?' Laura asked in a surprisingly calm voice and the mage hesitated.

'There are options open to you,' he said slowly. 'The curse would be weakened if you removed yourself to a world with a low magical field. There it would most likely represent itself not as full blindness but as a blurring or clouding of your vision. However there is a problem in that if you found a world to dwell where the magical field was greater than that of the Library the curse might spread and affect other senses besides your vision.'

'And those are my only options?' Laura asked.

'I am truly sorry,' Tan Ecesis told her. 'The mage who did this to you was obviously powerful. Otherwise I might be able to weaken the effects of the curse somewhat myself. Unfortunately there is nothing I can do.'

'What about another mage?' Alex asked, unable to help himself. 'Someone more competent at it.'

'I doubt that any are powerful enough to remove a curse so firmly set,' the mage said, looking a little annoyed. 'Although if the person who placed it on you could be persuaded to remove it . . . '

'That's unlikely,' Laura said curtly.

'Well, then. Perhaps if that person were dead, or came to regret the circumstances that gave rise to the original spell . . . ' his voice trailed off. 'I'm sorry I cannot help you further.'

Alex looked at Laura to see how she was taking the news and to his surprise she seemed as cool and collected as ever.

'That's all right,' she said, with the slightest of smiles. 'I understand and it was kind of you to see me. You've been very helpful.'

'It was the least I could do,' Tan Ecesis told her, his ruffled feelings soothed by her reply. 'Is there anything else I can help you with at all?'

'Actually, there is one thing,' Laura said. 'Just in case I do meet another mage, or any of those circumstances change, could you perhaps write your diagnosis down for me? It might come in useful.'

'Certainly,' the mage nodded. 'Happy to oblige. Should I write it in your book?'

'I don't have a book,' Laura said and he looked sorrowful.

'Oh, of course, well I'll find something,' he said. 'In fact I have a few blank notebooks of my own here. Permit me to bestow one upon you.'

They had to wait even longer while the mage ceremoniously produced a book and wrote out a lengthy explanation of Laura's blindness and Alex sighed with impatience. But it wasn't until they left the study that he asked his sister why she'd wanted the diagnosis.

'Do you want to get a second opinion or something?' he asked her.

'No, although if the opportunity arises I might do,' she said coolly, tucking the slim notebook away into a pocket of her long skirts. 'I simply thought some evidence might come in handy.'

'Evidence?' Alex frowned. 'You're blind, aren't you? Isn't that enough evidence for you?'

'Perhaps.' Laura shrugged her shoulders. 'But these people do everything by the book. Don't you think we should play by their rules?'

'I suppose so,' he agreed although he still didn't see much point in Laura keeping a magical medical record. 'What did you think about the other things he said? About how you could be cured if Morgan died or changed her mind about having cursed you?'

Laura didn't respond for a moment, walking smoothly down the corridor as if she wasn't blind at all, then she shrugged again.

'I don't think it's very likely she'll change her mind,' she said.

* * *

The Converse Court was the most impressive room Zoë had seen in the Library. The Crossway might have been larger but this was much more splendid and she looked around her with a kind of awe.

It was a wide open space twice the height of any ordinary room and the patterned wooden floor shone with reflected light. Zoë found her eyes drawn up to look for the source of the light and found it coming from hundreds of softly glowing spheres swirling around and about the high ceiling of the room. It took her a moment to drag her gaze back to the floor and when she did she noticed something she hadn't seen before. The wide polished floor was dotted with wooden pulpits, some large enough for four or five people, others only big enough for one, each with a few steps leading round the curved side of a pillar and a high railing around the standing room at the top. A few of these were occupied by a speaker and surrounded by a small group of listeners but most of the people in the room stood in knots clustered around and about the vast expanse of the floor. Around the perimeter of the room were several rows of elaborately carved wooden benches where groups of people sat together talking or eating or reading books.

Lisle Weft had brought them this far while Laura and Alex spoke with one of the Jurist magicians, her red-coated dog trotting obediently at her heels. But soon after showing them the room she'd excused herself, saying that she had other business to attend to, and they'd been left to explore.

They made their way around the room slowly, and after a few minutes Jhezra moved suddenly in surprise and touched Zoë's arm before pointing up above their heads. Two of the glowing spheres had detached themselves from the main mass and were following them about, bobbing like balloons as they trailed the two girls across the room.

'What are they?' Zoë asked in alarm, twisting her neck

uncomfortably as she tried unsuccessfully to step out from underneath the one above her.

'Some kind of magic, I think,' said Jhezra. 'But why should they follow us?'

'Look,' Zoë said, looking around the room. 'Everyone has one.' There were between fifty and a hundred people here and there in the Converse Court and every one of them had a glowing sphere following them. Those who were standing still had their sphere floating a couple of metres above their heads but if they moved about their spheres trailed a bit behind them at the same height.

'It doesn't look as if they're doing any harm,' Jhezra acknowledged. 'But it's strange to be followed by a magic spy.'

'It might just be a light,' Zoë said but she wondered if Jhezra might be right and that the globes were watching them.

However, after a while she didn't even notice her globe any more. There was too much to see. The people who thronged the Converse Court all seemed to be occupied in something or other. Some mounted the steps of a pulpit and started speaking, slowly gathering small groups of listeners and a cluster of glowing spheres above them. Others circulated the room carrying trays or bags of objects which they offered about like market traders and still more stood by the inevitable bookshelves which ringed the room, looking at books.

Zoë noticed that the volumes on each shelf had the same titles and stopped to point them out to Jhezra.

'Look how many of them are the same,' she said. 'All of this row are *Recent Journeys of the Peregrinades*, and there are three rows of *Scholar's Almanac* there and another two of *A Map to the Mapmakers*.' She stared at the rows of identical books wonderingly. 'It's like a bookshop,' she said.

'And see who is stocking the shelves,' Jhezra told her, drawing her attention to a gangling figure loading a set of books out of a knapsack and on to an empty shelf.

'Glossali Intergrade!' Zoë exclaimed and the young man looked up at the sound of his name. 'It's nice to see you again,' she said.

'Zoë, Jhezra,' Glossali said, with a correct little bow to each of them. 'Are Laura and Alex not with you?'

'We're going to meet them here,' Zoë explained. 'Laura's seeing a mage who might be able to help her eyesight.'

'Ah, well, I certainly hope she's successful,' Glossali said. 'In the meantime, may I offer you a book?'

Zoë found herself taking the book automatically and then had to suppress a smile as she showed it to Jhezra. The writing on the cover read: *The Cult of the Catalogue*.

'So, are all these books just free then?' Zoë asked and Glossali nodded.

'The Jurists invite factions to bring their history and manifests here, so that people can learn about us and join us if they wish.'

'Have you always been a Catalogue Cultist, Glossali?' Zoë asked, suddenly curious, and the young man nodded.

'I'm third generation Collegiate,' he said with an air of pride. 'My parents were Scholars before they joined the Catalogue Cult and my grandparents were Scholars on one side and Booksellers on the other.' As the two girls took this in he added: 'I've never spent a whole day outside the Library.'

'You say that as if it's a good thing,' Zoë said.

'I'm not surprised you find it strange,' Glossali told her, not taking offence. 'You have to be brought up to it to understand the Library.' Straightening his row of books neatly on the shelf he reached down for his half empty pack. 'Well, I must spread the word of the Catalogue Cult some more.' He gestured vaguely at the scattered pulpits. 'But perhaps we'll catch up with each other later. I hope you find the book useful.'

'Thank you!' Zoë said, feeling bad for wanting to laugh at him earlier and remembering how helpful he had been to bring them through the Library. 'I'll read it, I promise.' She watched as he waved a goodbye and then disappeared into the crowd before turning to Jhezra. 'Now I'll have to do it,' she commented, stuffing the book into her kitbag. 'And I bet it's dull as ditchwater.'

'Unfortunately, yes,' Jhezra agreed. 'But we should take some of the others also. It's strange, I never owned a book in my life and now I have a sudden urge to possess as many as I can.'

'The Library's getting to us,' Zoë agreed. 'I'm feeling that too. Everyone here's just fixated on books.'

But even though she tried not to take everything she saw, after only half an hour of looking at the shelves she was juggling six books in her arms and her bag was bulging with more.

'I think we're going to have to leave it there,' she said, as Jhezra handed her the latest find, an attractive peacock-blue book with pages of illuminated text and the title *Marvels of the Magi*. 'I can't carry much more and my arms are getting tired.'

'Perhaps we should listen to one of the speakers,' Jhezra suggested and Zoë nodded.

'OK,' she agreed. 'But please not Glossali. I think I've heard as much about the Catalogue Cult as I'm ever going to want to!'

Ciren and Charm passed guard-post twenty-three less than an hour after Morgan and Kal. They'd been travelling at a quick pace by then, certain they were gaining on the runaways as they questioned the corridor guards and watchers, and had only paused for a brief confirmation.

'We're following two fugitives,' Charm said to the leader of the guards. 'Have you seen them?' The question was almost irrelevant as she accompanied her question with a thin cold smile.

As her mind twined around the guardsman, discovering not only that he'd seen Kal and Morgan but had actually shown them a Wheel map and aided their escape, she stiffened with anger.

'We've seen two Collegiate members,' the guard said anxiously. 'Forgive me, we didn't know they were fugitives. Are you certain it's they you seek . . . ?'

'Of course it's them,' Charm said sharply and turned to her twin. 'These fools gave them directions beyond the Wheel section. They actually showed them a map.' Her voice dripped with contempt and Ciren looked unhappy.

'Show us the route you gave them,' he told the guardsman. 'If you aid us now it may count in your favour when your error is made known to the Council.'

'Certainly,' the guardsman said hastily, blanching at Ciren's expression and unnerved by Charm's apparent reading of his mind. 'They claimed to be heading for Cryptographer territory. We directed them around the edge of the Jurist section to get there . . . '

'Sir, shouldn't we ask these two for confirmation of their identity?' one of the other guards asked and Charm turned to berate him. But it was Ciren who spoke first with an unexpected anger in his voice, as if relieved to take out the frustration of the search on someone.

'It's a bit late for that now,' he said icily. 'I assure you we have any number of ways of proving our identity as genuine members of the Wheel but your incompetence leaves you unworthy of such a courtesy. Now tell us what we need to know quickly or my twin will rip it out of your mind.'

Charm's smile stretched as she felt a rush of happiness at the realization that Ciren was in agreement with her once more. As the guardsmen hurried to supply them with the information they needed she confirmed it by searching their memories. But this time there was no real need, they had been sufficiently cowed by the threat of being brought up before the Council on charges of incompetence.

Charm confiscated their maps before leaving and the guards stood in silence behind them as the twins headed up the staircase at the end of the corridor.

'I don't know much about this section,' she said. 'I know we have relations with the Cryptographers but who are the Jurists?'

'Law givers,' Ciren said ominously. 'They take the codes of the Collegiate more seriously than most and devote their energies to communicating with as many factions as they can. So far the Council has been careful not to let them know much about the Wheel; the last thing Vespertine would want is for them to meddle in our affairs.'

'Then we must make a plan for how we present ourselves to them,' Charm realized. 'Or they won't turn over Morgan and Kal to us.'

'It will be difficult,' Ciren said slowly. 'When we get there we must watch and wait for the right opportunity.'

'And then we'll strike,' Charm said with satisfaction and Ciren's eyes were empty as he agreed.

11

Alex hadn't found the Converse Court as easily as Lisle Weft had claimed he would. It was harder than people made out to keep track of all the turnings of the corridors in this place where everything looked the same. It would have been a damned sight easier to navigate if they had a decent system of signposts, he thought bitterly.

After they'd had to stop and ask for directions twice Laura had lost patience with him and had insisted that he describe every step of the way, asking constantly if they'd come to the next turn or landmark. It hadn't made him feel any more charitably towards her when this time they'd managed to find the place and had spilled out of an entrance way into a wide open hall that was obviously the Converse Court they'd been looking for. He'd almost been tempted to lie and say they hadn't got there yet but even Laura would be able to hear the voices of the mass of people wandering around the room.

It hadn't taken him long to spot Zoë and Jhezra

although they didn't seem to notice him. The two girls were standing near one of the strange podiums scattered around the room, apparently listening to a lecture. The speaker was a woman wearing a multicoloured dress of embroidered patchwork and a similar cloth bound through a waist-length plait of dark brown hair. A small crowd had gathered around her and there was a cluster of floating lights above her head as she harangued anyone who would listen.

'. . . they vanish into the dark,' she was saying as Alex guided Laura towards the others. 'Who here has heard of the dark sections where books and Library alike have been destroyed, leaving an empty void in their place? Who remembers the Lightbringers, or the Woodcarvers, or even the terror of the Gleaners, all of whom fell beneath factions more powerful who crushed them and left in their place burnt halls, broken books, and enslaved worlds?'

Alex rolled his eyes and bent his head to whisper to Laura. 'Some crank predicting doom and gloom.'

'I'm blind not deaf,' she snapped at him. 'And I want to listen.'

Alex sighed heavily and shifted uncomfortably. Laura seemed to have taken root where she stood and he couldn't be bothered to try and guide her around to where the others were. Meanwhile the woman on the podium seemed to be reaching her peroration.

'And who here can claim to know the Library?' she was saying, her voice pitched deep into the crowd. 'None of us can claim superiority over any initiated world-traveller while we still don't know why it exists. Who created the Collegiate? What force made the Doors which connect the universe with corridors of power? While we are ignorant of that we know nothing.'

'Speak for yourself!' a voice called out from among the listeners and a couple more people laughed. Alex grinned himself but the woman on the podium didn't seem to care.

'I do speak for myself,' she said. 'And for others whose words you would respect more. Caravaggion has warned you time and time again but you would not listen then either. We grow complacent here,' she went on and her voice was suddenly weary. 'Caravaggion said it, now I say it too. As of now I am once more a Peregrinade. I wish you well and hope that I may someday return to debate here with old friends and old enemies. But it is my fear that I will return to find nothing but echoless emptiness and the end of the Jurists.'

The woman stepped down from the podium and the listeners moved out of the way to let her pass, some pausing to speak with her and others drifting away to join groups around other lecturers. Around the ceiling lights bobbed and swung, following the patterns of motion in the room.

'Want to go find the others?' Alex asked and Laura's brows tightened in a frown half-concealed by the cloth that covered her eyes.

'In a minute,' she said irritably. 'Let me think.'

Alex was tempted for a moment just to leave her there if she couldn't be more grateful but just then he saw something that drew his attention instantly. Across the Converse Court was an archway leading to another corridor and there stood two people standing at the edges of the reflected light. Half in the shadows they seemed to be hiding from the crowd although their eyes scanned the room restlessly.

'Morgan!' he exclaimed out loud and Laura's whole body stiffened as her head lifted, and then turned eerily to stare across the room in the direction of the newcomers.

'She's here,' Laura said and Alex nodded, forgetting for a moment his sister was blind.

Morgan was dressed in black and in the alien surroundings of the Library she seemed abruptly menacing. Two of the glowing spheres were floating over to the new arrivals and the light they shed glinted suddenly on a tangle of spikes crowning the head of the figure next to Morgan and with another lurch of alarm Alex recognized the Archon of Shattershard.

Kal hadn't exactly followed the route the Wheel soldiers had suggested. He'd told Morgan it was too risky in case they were followed. So he'd suggested that instead of skirting the edge of Jurist territory that they make straight for it.

'If we don't trouble them, perhaps they won't trouble us,' he'd said to her.

She'd agreed but she was still feeling scared as they arrived at the entrance to what seemed to be a central meeting place. At least in the Wheel she'd known people from the faction and, until Kal had warned her against them, she'd trusted Ciren and Charm. Now she felt as if any stranger might be an enemy and she clung close to Kal's side as they entered the room.

It seemed to be a kind of debating chamber with several people standing on high pulpits and preaching to groups of interested listeners. But although several speakers were talking at once from different points in the room the noise was somehow muted and magical globes swam about softly shedding light on everyone inside. Morgan glanced from side to side as Kal forged his way through the crowd. She didn't know what she was looking for but when her eyes snagged on a tumbled mass of auburn curls she gasped in sudden surprise.

'Zoë!' As she spoke the red-headed girl turned to see who had spoken.

'What was that?' Kal asked and she pointed to where Zoë was now hurrying towards them, followed by another girl with dark hair and almond-shaped brown eyes. 'The Hajhi from the courtyard!' he exclaimed and his hand moved instinctively to the hilt of his sword.

'Morgan . . . ' Zoë came suddenly to a halt in front of her and the Hajhi girl stopped next to her, one hand moving towards her own weapons as she eyed them suspiciously. 'It's OK, Jhezra,' Zoë said quickly before looking back at Morgan and Kal. 'Thank God you're still alive. I can't believe you're here.'

'I thought you were dead,' Morgan told her. 'How did you manage to escape?'

'Through the Door you told me about,' Zoë said eagerly. 'The one underneath the City, remember? We went through it into the Library.'

'We?' Kal's voice was level as he turned to look from Zoë to Jhezra. 'You and this bandit?'

'I take exception to that term,' the Hajhi girl said angrily and Zoë looked from one to the other of them with an air of distress.

'Oh, don't,' she said. 'Please don't argue about it. Morgan, you have to listen . . . '

'It wasn't just you two, was it?' Morgan said, realizing what Zoë must be concealing. 'Laura and Alex escaped as well, didn't they?'

Kal's eyes went icy grey with anger and he turned his head to look about the room searchingly. Zoë was speaking again, trying to explain something, but Morgan wasn't listening to her. Like Kal she was turning and looking around, craning her neck to see across the room. Then she saw them. Alex was looking straight at them and next to him, her face half concealed by a brown silk scarf, was Laura Harrell.

* * *

Laura felt her face smooth over, concealing all expression behind a cool façade. Her hands trembled slightly and she raised them deliberately to smooth her hair back, patting it carefully into place until the tremors stopped. This was the moment she had anticipated and if she kept cool now, perhaps this time things would go her way.

She could sense Alex fidgeting beside her and she could practically feel his alarm. But she refused to let herself be distracted by it.

'They're looking at us,' he whispered urgently. 'Morgan and the Archon. Zoë's trying to talk to them but they're ignoring her. Jhezra looks as if she's about to go for her sword . . . '

'Take me to them,' Laura said smoothly.

'You have to be kidding,' Alex said. 'That bloke's already sliced me up once. I'm not going over there.'

'Don't be ridiculous,' Laura said, a snap of annoyance in her voice at her brother's lack of dignity. 'You know he can't do anything to us here. Remember what Glossali told us about the laws of the Library?'

'I know that, but does he?' Alex said mulishly but Laura had run out of patience.

'Come *on*,' she demanded, tugging at his sleeve.

'All right, already.' Taking her arm Alex began to steer her across the floor. 'But you had better know what you're doing, Laura.'

As they walked across the floor Laura could hear raised voices ahead and despite her confidence she was conscious of a certain anxiety. The worst of being blind was that you were vulnerable to physical attacks. If someone shoved or pushed her she wouldn't be able even to dodge. But she collected herself, remembering that in Shattershard she'd been vulnerable anyway to anyone with a weapon and yet she'd still managed to prosper there, and being able to see hadn't helped her against Morgan's magic.

She might be blind but at least she could rely on her intuition and she held her head up straight as she walked across the floor.

'Can't we put this behind us?' she could hear Zoë saying plaintively. 'Haven't we all been through enough by now? If you could just listen . . . '

'No, you must listen,' a firm commanding voice informed her and Laura recognized it as belonging to Kal, Shattershard's Archon. 'Whoever you are. These friends of yours have destroyed my home and killed many of my people. I will not be silent.'

'And what of our own dead?' Jhezra was demanding. 'Those killed by your Tetrarchate. What about my friends Vaysha and Tzandrian?'

'Kal, don't blame Zoë,' Morgan said. 'It's Laura and Alex who're responsible.'

'Oh very nice,' Alex said sarcastically, although Laura could feel him shaking with nerves. 'That's right, blame us for everything!'

'But it was your fault!' Morgan said hotly. 'You and Laura . . . ' She came suddenly to a halt and Laura turned her head towards the sound of her voice.

'Hello, Morgan,' Laura said, her voice very steady. 'As you can see you didn't manage to kill me. Are you going to try to finish the job?'

There was a shocked silence and Laura could hear it spreading around them like a pool of water. The murmur of other voices had died down and she could almost feel the heads turning in their direction.

'If she won't, I will,' Kal said grimly and Laura winced at the sound of metal grating with a sudden rasp.

'No!' Zoë shouted and a hubbub of voices rose around them.

'Stay back,' Jhezra called out and another sliding groan of metal made it clear she'd drawn her own weapons.

'Oh shit,' Alex cursed and Laura felt him jostle her as he tried to take a step back.

It was time. Things had come out almost exactly as Laura had anticipated. Perhaps this meeting had come earlier than she'd expected but that just showed how clever she'd been to prepare for it. Taking a deep breath she took a step away from the conflict, opened her mouth, and screamed.

Laura's scream cut through the room like a knife blade. Whatever magical acoustics controlled the level of the speakers' voices obviously wasn't equipped to cope with anything so loud. If anything the scream was magnified and Zoë shuddered as the end of it trailed away.

Everyone in the room had turned to stare at them and a ring of space was spreading around them as people backed away.

'Someone stop them!' a voice shouted in sudden outrage. 'They're going to try and finish her off this time.' Then Glossali Intergrade pushed his way through the crowd and hurried to Laura's side, putting a sympathetic arm around her shoulders as he turned to regard Morgan with a kind of horrified disgust. 'For God's sake, haven't you done enough harm?' he demanded.

'Me?' Morgan's voice was almost inaudible under the sudden murmur of confused enquiries breaking out around the room. As if Glossali's interruption had broken a spell people were moving in from all sides and one of them, a tall man whose black hair was faintly streaked with white, turned to step between the two groups.

'What exactly is the problem here?' he asked in a voice of stern command. 'No Collegiate member should draw weapons against another. Certainly not here in the Converse Court of the Jurists. Explain yourselves immediately.'

'These people destroyed my home and murdered my people,' the Archon of Shattershard claimed angrily. His sword was still in his hand and with it he described a half circle pointing at Alex, Jhezra, Zoë, and Laura. 'Is there no justice in this Library?'

'There is justice,' the tall stranger said. 'But not vengeance. Put your weapon away.' He turned to look at Jhezra. 'And you also. There will be no duelling here.'

'Will we have a chance to defend ourselves?' Jhezra asked, unafraid, although she returned her sickle and scimitar to their sheaths.

'Naturally you will,' a new voice said and Zoë looked up with relief to see Lisle Weft stepping out of the crowd. 'And it appears that we should proceed with haste if you young people are not to murder each other right here.' She frowned at them with disapproval. 'But you didn't say anything about this Archon's accusation when you came to see me earlier today.'

'That's because it isn't true,' Laura said, looking up from where she was leaning on Glossali Intergrade's arm. 'It's them who should be on trial, not us.'

'For drawing steel on each other and preparing to fight you all might be tried in this court,' the man who'd first broken up the argument pointed out. 'Don't worry, young lady, you'll be able to have your say.'

'Just bear in mind that everything she says is a lie,' Morgan said bitterly, glaring at Laura across the room.

'That's enough, now.' Lisle Weft spoke sharply. Looking around at each of them in turn she continued, 'I am Lisle and this is my colleague Dalandran. Whatever bloody and violent history lies between you young people must cease now. It is against the customs of the Collegiate and the ancient laws of the Library. Here in the presence of your equals your case will be considered and a fair judgement given by the Converse Court of the Jurists. Do you understand and accept this?'

Zoë bit her lips anxiously, looking around the room, and it was with shock that she realized that many of the Collegiate members that surrounded them were regarding her with curious suspicion. Lisle looked directly at her as she asked again, 'Do you understand and accept this?'

'Yes,' Zoë said in a small voice and Jhezra took a step closer to her in a gesture of support.

'I understand and will submit to the judgement of your court,' she said and bowed; but one of her hands remained on the hilt of her sword.

'Me too, I suppose,' Alex said, eyeing the Archon's sword warily.

'I agree,' Morgan said.

'I will agree to a fair trial of our case,' the Archon added, lifting his head proudly.

'And you?' Lisle asked, looking at where Laura stood leaning on Glossali a little apart from the others.

'Yes.' Laura's voice was faint but gained strength gradually. 'I understand and agree. I ask for nothing better than the judgement of the Jurists.'

But as Lisle led them away, Zoë couldn't escape the sense that Laura had been expecting this all along.

They didn't have long to wait. Zoë guessed that in a place like the Library where Collegiate members could be worlds away from each other, quarrels needed to be solved swiftly. But it was still alarming to see how swiftly the Converse Court arranged itself for a trial.

There were no lawyers. Lisle Weft explained the process to them and Zoë thought it sounded more like a military court martial than a jury trial. Six members of the Jurists including Lisle herself would be judge and jury. They would listen to the evidence and then decree a verdict.

'What sort of verdict?' Zoë asked nervously, wondering what kind of peculiar punishments the Collegiate might have for breaking their rules, and Lisle gave her a look of reassurance.

'Nothing too dreadful, I promise,' she said. 'Especially for anyone whose only fault was ignorance of our rules. And remember that the Collegiate do not kill.'

'Of course.' Alex looked instantly relieved and Zoë felt a cloud lifting from her feelings. She'd forgotten that the Jurists would have to abide by their own rules.

'All you have to do is tell your stories to the Court,' Lisle explained. 'I and the other Jurists may ask you questions, as may anyone else present in the Court. But as long as you speak truthfully all will go well.'

'What happens to people who lie?' Laura asked and Lisle turned to regard her narrowly. But Laura's face was half hidden behind her scarf and even Zoë couldn't make out her expression.

'The magic of the court will be able to tell if you knowingly lie,' she said. 'Differences of opinion are another matter and that is what we are here to judge.'

Throughout Lisle's explanation Morgan and the Archon, Kal, had stood a little apart from the rest of them. When the Court was eventually called to order each of them was directed to take a pulpit and Zoë saw Morgan flinch, reaching out to cling to Kal.

'Do we have to be separated?' she whispered and Lisle looked at her with sympathy.

'No,' she said, pointing out one of the pillars large enough to hold two speakers. 'You can take that place.' She looked around at the rest of them and asked: 'Do any of the rest of you want to stay together?'

'I'll be all right,' said Laura, surprisingly quickly given that she'd been leaning on Glossali Intergrade until then.

Alex looked at Jhezra and Jhezra raised her eyebrows at Zoë and Zoë shrugged.

'I'll be fine on my own,' she said, in case Jhezra wanted to stand with her former boyfriend. But Jhezra didn't.

'I need no support,' she said and Alex was left on his own.

'I'm not worried,' he said with bravado and a slight sneer in Morgan and Kal's direction.

'Very well then,' Lisle told them. 'Ascend to your places.'

She herself went back to the group of the other five judges who had claimed one of the larger podiums with a hexagon-shaped railing on which were mounted six wooden lecterns for resting books. Around the hall the audience gathered, mostly in between the witnesses and judges, and looked expectantly up at them. There were more people here now than there had been when Zoë had first arrived and she wondered if they'd been drawn by news of some drama in progress or if this was natural for the Converse Court.

The light spheres swirled around and about as people found good positions and Zoë wondered what happened if they ever didn't have enough for everyone there. But looking up into the heights of the hall she could see many more clustered than were in use, their light dimmed to a faint glow. The six lights floating above the judges lit them up clearly and the two above Morgan and Kal gleamed on the Archon's crown almost as brightly; but even with only one drifting above her head Zoë felt very exposed standing up on a pulpit where anyone could see her.

As the audience quietened down and Lisle prepared to speak, Zoë took a deep breath. She thought about her dad and how he'd want to be proud of her, even in a weird situation like this. She knew what Kal would probably accuse Laura and Alex of and although she didn't want to get them into trouble she was determined that she wouldn't lie to protect them either. After all, it wasn't as if anything really bad would happen to them. Lisle had promised that.

Kal was surprised that he and Jhezra, the Hajhi warrior, had been allowed to keep their weapons. He suspected that the fact they had been allowed to keep them meant that the court wasn't worried about any physical threat and glancing up at the floating lights he had an idea what might be the defence against a magical attack. He fervently hoped that the Court would be fair because it looked as if they might have trouble evading its verdict if it wasn't.

Lisle Weft, the elderly woman who seemed to be in charge of the proceedings, cleared her throat and announced:

'The Converse Court commences. The matter open for our consideration is the dispute between these five young people. They have given their names as Kal khi Kalanthé, Morgan, Alex-Iskander Harrell, Laura Harrell, Zoë Kaul, and Jhezra Jhazrhi Hajhim. Who among you wishes to speak first?'

Kal didn't hesitate. He wanted to make the issues plain to everyone concerned and he was confident of his own abilities as a speaker. The Harrells and their friends had destroyed his city and he was determined to prove it to these people. Although his first thought on seeing Alex had been to cut him down with his sword, a trial actually suited him even better. He wanted to see the criminals brought to justice and perhaps after that set these Jurists on the Wheel.

'I will speak,' he said clearly. 'If no one has any objection.'

'Very well, then,' Lisle nodded. 'You may commence.'

'Thank you.' Kal bowed very slightly to the panel of judges and then to the audience. 'Jurists and other members of the Collegiate, thank you for hearing me. My name is Kal and until recently I was the Archon of a city named Shattershard . . . '

As he told his tale he spoke as plainly as he could. He told them about Shattershard's precarious position on the borderland between the desert and the Tetrarchate empire. He explained how hostilities had grown up between Shattershard's citizens, the Tetrarchate troops, and the desert-dwelling Hajhim. Then he told the story of the battle. How Alex and Jhezra had led the Hajhim into the city and launched other-world weapons against the citizens and the Tetrarchate soldiers and how those weapons had brought the city down.

'With the help of my companion, Morgan, I escaped the city even as earthquakes shook it to pieces around us,' he concluded. 'In the final battle I had wounded the Harrell boy when I was attacked by the Hajhi girl who calls herself Jhezra. Until now I thought them and their associates dead. Since they live, I'm relieved to discover that they are to face justice for their crimes. If what I've been told of the laws of the Collegiate is true, these people have broken them many times over.'

When the Archon came to the end of his speech there were grim murmurs from the audience and Alex looked about indignantly. Kal had actually made it sound as if everything was his fault. When Lisle asked if one of them would like to speak in their defence he stood up straight.

'I'd like to say something!' he said and waited

impatiently for Lisle to glance around at the others and then finally signal that he might begin.

Alex had been a bit surprised that Laura hadn't wanted to stand with him. But now that it came to it he actually liked the attention of being there on his own without his sister hanging on his arm. He actually enjoyed having the instant attention of everyone in the hall.

'What happened in Shattershard was a lot more complicated than the Archon is making it sound,' he told them. 'And it would be unfair to judge us by Collegiate rules since we didn't know anything about them until coming here. Basically, when we found a Door from our world into the desert outside Shattershard, the Hajhim told us how much the Tetrarchate had mistreated their people. When I fought with the Hajhi warriors it was to help gain their freedom from an oppressive and evil empire and I had no idea Shattershard was so poorly constructed that the weapons we used would collapse the city. Obviously if I had we wouldn't have planted them where we did.'

He came to a halt and realized that his defence of himself had ended rather quickly. But as he went over the points again he couldn't really think of much to add. Basically, they hadn't known the rules and they hadn't meant to destroy Shattershard and if the Tetrarchate hadn't been so oppressive they wouldn't have needed to attack the city in the first place. But the audience didn't seem to be satisfied.

'Even if you hadn't destroyed the city, the weapons you used must have killed many people anyway. Don't you feel some guilt for that?' someone called out from the floor and Lisle indicated he had to answer.

'It was a war,' Alex said. 'People die in wars.' He paused for a second and added, 'And it wasn't us who started the war. The Tetrarchate and the Hajhim were already at odds when we arrived in Shattershard.'

'But why did you join in?' one woman asked and Alex lifted his hands helplessly.

'We were friends with the Hajhim,' he said and turned to look at Jhezra. 'We wanted to help them.'

'It didn't occur to you to try to bring about peace?' someone else asked and Alex glared down at the dimly lit questioner.

'How am I supposed to answer that?' he demanded and then turned to Lisle. 'That's an impossible question.'

Lisle looked troubled but she waved the questioner down and looked around at the rest of the audience.

'Are there any further questions?' she asked and although there were mutters and murmurs no one seemed to want to ask anything more.

'Excuse me?' a voice asked and Alex was surprised to see that Kal had leant forward from his podium and raised a hand. 'May I say something?'

'If you are brief,' Lisle said. 'You were given ample opportunity to speak earlier.'

'Thank you.' Kal bowed to her before fixing Alex with a cold look. 'Alex Harrell claims he attacked the city because we were responsible for persecuting the Hajhim. This isn't true. Shattershard was an independent city. My people did not support or condone the Tetrarchate government.'

'That's not true!' Alex objected and to his relief he saw Jhezra nodding.

'No, it is not,' she told the court, turning to look around at everyone. 'Alex supported my people because we needed his help. We were constantly being pushed back into the deeper desert by guards from the city and by soldiers from the Tetrarchate empire. We were not permitted to trade freely or even to remain within the city walls without a sponsor to vouch for our good behaviour. All my life the Tetrarchate gained more control and it was getting worse, not better. Officially the Archon might have ruled Shattershard but it was the Tetrarchate who were really in charge as we saw when their soldiers came to defend the walls and to attack us in the desert. The city dwellers did nothing to stop them.'

'We couldn't!' Kal protested, losing some of his dignity in his insistence. 'The Tetrarchate were too powerful.'

'You allied with them to protect yourselves,' Jhezra declared, facing Kal across the heads of the onlookers. 'And in allying with them you oppressed us.'

'No, it's not true,' Kal said again but he didn't sound as certain and this time Lisle silenced him.

'You've had your chance to speak,' she said. 'It would appear that the two of you view the situation very differently.' She frowned in thought and then turned to speak in low tones to the other Jurists.

Alex tried to catch Jhezra's eye while they waited but she was still watching Kal. Her expression was distant and she stared at the Archon as if she was trying to look inside his thoughts. From his own pulpit Kal returned her look but he didn't look as confident as he had and Alex hoped that Jhezra's testimony had dealt a blow to his case.

'With the city destroyed far away from here and the people scattered we are uncertain of how to reach the truth here,' the tall man who had called himself Dalandran announced. 'I don't believe any of these people could be considered an independent witness.'

'Um,' a small sound broke the silence. 'I think I can.' Zoë stood up very straight but one of her hands fiddled nervously with a strand of her hair. 'I was only in Shattershard for a week,' she said quietly. 'I didn't have time to join anyone's side even if I'd wanted to.'

12

Laura heard Zoë's declaration and had to remind herself that people were watching her in order not to let her feelings get the better of her. Sometimes she felt that travelling with Zoë was like rolling for luck in a role-playing game. On the one hand the red-headed girl had known a way out of Shattershard and been easy to persuade to explore the Library. But on the other hand her insistence on detail when explaining herself was rather too zealously literal for Laura's liking.

Zoë's behaviour was an element that Laura couldn't predict. If she could have thought of a way of getting her silenced during this mocked-up trial she'd have done it but unfortunately Zoë always ended up in the thick of things. But Laura was now confident she understood the workings of the Converse Court and there might be worse times for Zoë to speak her piece. So Laura held still and listened in silence.

'I really don't know much about the politics of

Shattershard,' Zoë was saying. 'But I think I'm about as independent a witness as you can get. The Harrells and Morgan had been travelling there for years and Jhezra and Kal lived there. I only saw it for the first time . . . ' she paused and there was a note of disbelief in her voice as she continued, 'about three weeks ago. I can't believe how much has happened since then.'

There was a light sound of laughter here and there in the room and Laura thought it sounded sympathetic. Zoë obviously made a good witness.

'My name's Zoë,' Zoë went on after a moment. 'I should probably have said that before. Anyway I was in the same class as Laura at school and she showed me the Door through to Shattershard . . . '

As Zoë told her story, Laura could tell from the quality of the silence that she had everyone's attention. The way she explained her own wonder and confusion meant that the audience sympathized with her and her story rang with the note of truth as she explained what had happened in the city.

'I don't know how much Shattershard was under the thumb of the Tetrarchate,' she admitted. 'But I do know that it was at least officially independent. Tetrarchate troops wore blue and silver uniforms but the city guards of Shattershard wore grey. The last time I went inside the city there were both kinds of guards at the gate but before there'd only been the grey ones.' Her voice choked up a bit as she added: 'My dad's a soldier back on my world so I notice things like that . . . '

Zoë took a moment to recover herself and Laura could practically hear the audience's sympathy rolling out in waves from the crowd. It really wasn't fair of Zoë to turn the story into such a tear jerker just because she missed her father. After all, no one had forced her to come through the Door.

'Anyway,' Zoë said, recovering herself, 'I don't think what was going on between the Tetrarchate and the Hajhim is really the point. You see, when the city fell in everyone was still fighting. The city guards and the Tetrarchate troops and the Hajhi warriors and some of us . . . I don't know who would have won or what would have happened if the battle had come to an end in a normal way.' She took a deep breath and went on.

'But the city fell in then and it collapsed because Alex planted bombs in the tunnels beneath the gates. Jhezra and some of the other Hajhim helped because he told them it would stop the gates from closing. And it did. But it also messed up the complicated hydraulic system underneath the mountain and that's what destroyed the city.'

'That was Alex's fault,' Zoë concluded slowly. 'And Laura's.'

There was silence in the Converse Court and Laura knew that people had turned to look at her. She wasn't surprised that no one had questioned Zoë and she'd been expecting this moment ever since Alex had told her Morgan was here.

'Laura Harrell?' Lisle Weft asked. 'Would you like to speak now?'

Laura drew a slow calm breath and rested her hands lightly on the rail of the pulpit, lifting her head and directing her words a little to the left of where she thought the judges were.

'When Alex and Morgan and I found the Door into Shattershard we'd never heard of the Collegiate,' she began. 'We didn't know about the rule that forbids world-travellers to reveal their origins but even so we realized it would cause problems to tell the truth. So I posed as a merchant trader. I brought cheap trinkets from our world and sold them in the city. But Alex and Morgan were more ambitious.'

Laura almost smiled but caught herself. She couldn't let herself look triumphant. Not yet. But the rhythm of her words was convincing and she wondered if the others had begun to guess what her plan was.

'Alex wanted to be a warrior,' she said. 'He formed a relationship with the Hajhim and with Jhezra.' This time she did smile and there were murmurs around the hall. 'Morgan wanted to be a magician and she joined the city guild of mages and later came to form a relationship with Kal, the city's Archon.'

Morgan's relationship with Kal hadn't happened until long after Alex's with Jhezra but Laura drew out the parallel. The implication was sufficient. Alex was linked to the tribes and Morgan was linked to the city.

'At this point in time the Hajhim were, as Jhezra told you, forbidden to enter or trade in the city without a sponsor. But I traded with both the people in Shattershard and the Hajhim. A trade that came to include books about martial arts, warfare, and strategy.'

'What about the weapons?' a voice called out from the floor and Laura turned her head this way and that as if trying to locate the speaker before fixing on a spot near where the voice had sounded and smiling.

'Please,' she said gently. 'In our world Alex and I were considered children. We wouldn't have been capable of bringing weapons. The Hajhim built those weapons themselves, using information from books we brought through the Door. Books that in our world were children's texts about the principles of matter manipulation.'

'But you did plan the attack on the city?' someone asked from the judge's podium and Laura shook her head.

'The plan was Alex's idea,' she told them. 'He was the one with the scientific knowledge and the Hajhim connections. It was his idea to use bombs to jam the gates. I thought it would mean a quick takeover and he'd promised that Kal wouldn't be harmed once the Hajhim held the city.'

Laura bent her head and then slowly lifted it again, leaning against the side of the pulpit wearily.

'Members of the Collegiate,' she said softly. 'Look at me. I'm a fifteen-year-old girl. I can't use a sword, I'm not strong, I don't know anything about fighting. I couldn't even defend myself before and now I'm blind.' She took a long slow breath. 'In the final battle Morgan turned against me, using her magic on behalf of Shattershard's Archon, and casting a spell that was supposed to kill me but instead left me as you can see . . . '

There was a rustle of movement around the room and Laura wished she could see the look on Morgan's face right now as she reached up and pulled the silk scarf away from her blinded eyes.

'Morgan knew your laws then as well as she does now,' she concluded, raising her voice to be heard across the room. 'Zoë can bear witness to that. Morgan had met Collegiate members although she told us nothing about them and they had told her the secrets of the Doors and the Library.' Laura lifted her head and this time she stared sightlessly at where she knew the Jurists to be. 'She knew your laws,' she said. 'And she blinded me and left me for dead.'

There was uproar in the Converse Court. Everyone seemed to be asking questions at once. Dazed by what had just happened Morgan heard Zoë reluctantly admitting that what Laura said was true and then being overruled as she tried to protest that it wasn't the whole truth.

'Laura hasn't lied,' Lisle said firmly. 'And Morgan will have her chance to defend herself. Now.'

She didn't realize she was shaking until Kal stroked

her back to calm her and then she felt as if she couldn't stop. Her first words came out as inaudible stammers and she had to stop talking to try and keep hold of herself.

'Don't worry,' Kal whispered gently. 'They won't hurt you, remember? It will be all right.'

'Morgan?' Lisle's voice was firm. 'You must speak. You have to defend yourself.'

'I'm sorry,' Morgan managed to say. 'Just give me a moment.'

Lisle nodded but the other Jurists looked stern and everyone in the court was watching her and the expressions on their faces weren't gentle. Morgan knew what Laura had done although she was sure there was no way she could explain it. Their class had studied *Julius Caesar* last year and Laura had read Mark Antony's speech, the one which started out praising the hero and ended by turning everyone against him. Laura had turned the whole situation to her advantage and made herself look like the victim and Morgan didn't know how she could get people to believe it wasn't true.

Faltering, she started to tell the story of how she'd come to Shattershard and what it had felt like to discover that she had real magic.

'We don't have magic in my world,' she explained. 'And I was never really good at anything before. But in Shattershard I felt like I was special.'

She told them about Alex and Laura's dealings with the tribes and how she'd been sure they were planning something, so sure that she'd warned Zoë against them. But coming after Laura's testimony her own words sounded thin and hollow even to herself. She tried to explain that she hadn't told Kal or the twins about Alex and Laura because she'd still felt loyal to them but she knew she wasn't being convincing.

'Who are these twins anyway?' Dalandran asked from

the judges' box. 'If they were Collegiate members what faction were they from?'

'It's called the Wheel,' Morgan told them.

'The Wheel?' Lisle said sharply.

'We're not members of it,' Morgan tried to explain. 'They helped me and Kal escape from Shattershard and they took us to the Tetrarchate capital city and through a Door there into the Library. But we ran away.'

'Did they tell you our laws?' a voice called from the floor and Morgan twisted her hands together helplessly.

'They did but I didn't think about them during the battle,' she tried to explain. 'Kal was fighting and I wanted to get to him and then Laura grabbed me and pulled my hair.' Someone actually laughed then and Lisle ordered silence. 'I wasn't trying to kill her,' Morgan pleaded. 'At least I don't think I was. I didn't even mean to cast a spell. I was just so angry and then this black cloud came out of me and covered Laura. That's all that happened. I didn't know it would blind her.'

There were more questions but she couldn't answer them. Hunched in the pulpit she groped for Kal's hand and felt him squeeze it tightly. His face was grey with worry though when she looked at him and she knew she'd made a bad witness. She had to cling on to his assurance that they wouldn't punish her too harshly but she dreaded what the verdict would be.

In a daze Morgan heard Lisle Weft declare that the time for speaking was over and that the judges would now retire to consider their verdict and if anyone had any further evidence it should be brought to them privately. Her eyes were blurry as she saw the young stranger who had been standing with Laura earlier follow after them carrying a thin notebook and she wondered how he was going to turn the knife further. It hardly mattered, she already knew that Laura had won.

* * *

Zoë didn't feel able to speak to Laura after what had just happened. Hurrying down the stairs from her pulpit she went to join Jhezra and the Hajhi girl clasped her hands in hers.

'Zoë, I'm sorry,' Jhezra said. 'You seem upset.'

'Morgan's not to blame,' Zoë insisted in a fierce whisper. 'I know that she was on the other side from you but you have to believe me.'

'I do believe you,' Jhezra said instantly. 'And I trust your judgement; but it's not me you have to convince.'

Zoë looked in the direction of the room Lisle and the other Jurists had disappeared to and saw Glossali Intergrade returning. Laura and Alex were standing together on the other side of the hall from Morgan and Kal and before Glossali could go and join them, Zoë called him over.

'Glossali!' she said. 'What did you go to the judges for?'

'Laura asked me to take them the mage's diagnosis of her blindness,' the young Catalogue Cultist explained. 'So they know all the details.'

'How very helpful of her,' Zoë said bitterly and Glossali looked surprised.

'Aren't you pleased?' he asked. 'Laura's attacker will certainly be brought to justice now. The Jurists will never tolerate such a blatant breach of the Collegiate code.'

'Oh, God.' Zoë stared at him. 'You've been planning this all along, haven't you? All the things you told us about the rules. It was all to help Laura get vengeance on Morgan. I can't believe it . . . You're as much her pawn as anyone in Shattershard!'

'Zoë, be calm,' Jhezra said. 'Glossali was only trying to help.'

But Zoë turned away and with an expression of hurt Glossali left them and went back to join Laura and Alex. It wasn't really him she blamed though. She felt as if she should have seen this coming and she blamed herself that she hadn't. Morgan had once warned her that Laura lied. This time she'd managed to do it by telling the truth.

They waited with the rest of the audience in the Converse Court for the judges to arrive at their verdict. It didn't take long. Within an hour they had returned to their places on the large pulpit and Dalandran turned to address the court.

'We have come to a decision on the fate of these young people whose tragic history we have all heard today,' he said. 'I will take each of them in order.'

Zoë was surprised when the stern looking man turned towards her first and unbent a little to smile at her.

'Zoë Kaul,' he said, 'the judges consider you to have been called only as a witness since you are clearly innocent of any wrong doing. No act of yours contributed to the disaster.'

From beside him Lisle Weft added, 'You are free to go wherever you will and the Jurists wish you better fortune the next time you travel the worlds.'

'Thank you,' Zoë said, nonplussed.

Moving on to regard first Kal and then Jhezra with a piercing look, Dalandran continued his verdict.

'We next turn our attention to Kal khi Kalanthé, the Archon of Shattershard, and Jhezra Jhazrhi, warrior of the Hajhim. In the opinion of the judges the situation of these two witnesses is curiously symmetrical. Furthermore, since neither of them were world-travellers at the time these events occurred they can only fairly be judged by the terms of their own world.'

'We will hold their speeches on record should anyone else involved in this affair come before this Court,' Lisle said, gesturing to a book in front of the Jurists.

'Come forward,' Dalandran said, and Kal and Jhezra came up slowly to stand in front of the judges' pulpit. 'The Jurists enjoin you to remember that you are world-travellers now and the laws of the Collegiate forbid you to carry on this ancient antagonism.' He paused and Lisle added:

'Do the two of you swear to lay this enmity aside?'

Kal and Jhezra looked at each other and the rest of the court watched them. Finally Jhezra bowed her head in a gesture of respect.

'Let there be peace between us,' she said. 'Too many of our people are dead and our world is far away.'

'I agree,' Kal said and his voice was weary. 'I'm not your enemy and never was. I swear I won't take any action against you from now on.'

Dalandran looked on as Kal and Jhezra returned to their places. Then he paused for a while and murmurings in the audience died down as he addressed the court at large.

'Alex-Iskander and Laura Harrell present a more difficult problem,' he began. 'Although they knew nothing of the Collegiate, they did take information and items from one world and used them to gain influence in another. This, however, is an offence that different factions judge differently and trafficking in commonly available books at least is no offence.' He paused and then looked directly at Alex, making him the focus of a cold stare. 'Alex-Iskander,' he said, 'you not only brought books, you assisted in the production of engines of destruction and were responsible for how they were put to use. You may not have planned the destruction that occurred but you remain responsible for many deaths for which you appear to feel no remorse.'

'But . . . ' Alex began but Dalandran's remorseless voice overrode him.

'In the judgement of the Jurists you should be returned to your home world or the nearest suitable equivalent and banned from world-travelling for a period of no less than twenty years until you are judged to have grown up.'

'What the hell!' Alex exclaimed as the audience erupted in uproar and Zoë watched in shock. She hadn't imagined that the punishment might be anything like this.

Alex continued to object until two Jurists took charge of him and told him if he wasn't quiet by choice he would be silenced. Then Dalandran looked at Laura and voices murmured just below the edge of hearing from around the Court.

'We now come to consider Laura, whose case is irretrievably intermingled with that of Morgan,' he stated.

Zoë, watching, noticed to her alarm that none of the judges had so much as glanced at Morgan since returning to the court; a very bad sign. Meanwhile Dalandran was directing his comments partly to Laura and partly to the audience.

'Laura's activities in Shattershard were primarily those of a merchant,' he began. 'In fact she traded with the city and with the desert people. She had no military or scientific knowledge of her own and trusted her brother's judgement that the plan would open the gates and bring a quick defeat to the city. She had no plan to harm the Archon and hoped for a bloodless victory.'

Zoë was sure that wasn't true but she couldn't prove it and Dalandran was still speaking.

'Furthermore,' he said, 'whatever wrongs Laura might have committed she has been more than punished. Evidence of Tan Ecesis, mage of this section, has been presented to the judges showing that Laura has little to no hope of recovering her vision. Therefore, we have decided that Laura be judged free from any further reprisal and we enjoin her to find a more experienced world-traveller to guide her actions and help her cope with her disability.'

Laura smiled and Zoë clenched her fists tight. Laura had caused trouble that she'd never even imagined possible and got away with it. She wondered what kind of disability Laura's blindness really was since it didn't seem to stop her causing mayhem wherever she went.

The rest of the audience were talking amongst themselves and Lisle Weft had to wave them down to silence again.

'There is the chance that Morgan might be able to remove the curse she put on Laura,' she said and she turned to meet Morgan's frightened eyes. 'Morgan? Will you remove the spell?'

'I'm sorry,' Morgan stammered. 'I don't . . . I don't think I can. I don't even know what I did.' Her hands were shaking as she concluded, 'I suppose I could try . . .'

'With respect to the rest of the judges, I don't advise it,' Dalandran said coldly. 'If Morgan still feels antagonism towards Laura, and it would appear that she does, such an attempt might exacerbate the spell rather than remove it.'

'I'm sorry,' Morgan whispered. But she looked at the floor and not at Laura.

'Morgan.' Lisle's voice was very gentle. 'Are you prepared to accept the judgement of the court?'

'Does she have any choice?' Kal asked, putting an arm around Morgan, and his voice was harsh with concern.

'She does not,' Dalandran said. 'What is more, at any sign that she intends to use her magic she will be suppressed.' Morgan stared at him, her eyes wide, as if she couldn't believe what he was suggesting.

'I won't use magic,' she said faintly. 'I'll accept what you decide.'

'Very well then.' It was Dalandran who announced the verdict. 'On your own world you had no magic. Now you have it but by your own admission cannot control it. In the opinion of all civilized factions a rogue mage is a danger to herself and to everyone around her. Therefore this court orders you to return to your own world and to remain there for ever.'

Morgan looked as if she was about to faint and Kal had to support her, as he glared angrily at the Jurists. But Dalandran was not yet finished.

'Does anyone here know a route back to this girl's home world?' he asked and suddenly two voices spoke in unison out of the crowd:

'We do.'

Kal turned to look. Everything around him seemed to have slowed down so that an eternity passed as he watched the twin figures walk out of the audience.

'I am Ciren,' the first said with a polite bow. 'And this is my twin.'

'My name is Charm,' she said and smiled.

Morgan's expression was terrified and Kal swallowed quickly, trying to find the words to convince the judges that this was a terrible mistake.

'Not them,' he said hoarsely. 'They're from the Wheel. We were escaping their faction when we arrived here.'

'Is this true?' Lisle asked, eyeing the twins narrowly, and Ciren looked reproachfully at Kal.

'It's true they were leaving us,' he said. 'Although we had hoped to persuade them otherwise. But the Wheel is innocent of any wrongdoing.'

'We listened to the trial,' Charm said with the same

sweet smile on her lips. 'We're the Collegiate members Laura mentioned before.' She turned to look at Laura with open interest. 'The ones who taught Morgan the rules of the Collegiate and rescued her and Kal from the destruction of Shattershard.'

'We would have liked to rescue these others as well,' Ciren added. 'But we barely escaped with our lives as it was.'

'And we brought Morgan and Kal back with us to the Library so we could teach Morgan how to use her magic,' Charm concluded.

Dalandran frowned and then turned to look at Morgan, who was shaking in Kal's arms.

'Is this true?' he asked.

'Yes but . . . ' Morgan faltered and Kal spoke for her.

'The Wheel is dangerous,' he said clearly. 'They wanted Morgan's magic for their own purposes. They're using their influence to control hundreds of worlds.'

'Do you have any proof of this?' Dalandran asked doubtfully and Kal was left at a loss. 'Well, is this true?' the tall man went on, looking at the twins, and Ciren shrugged expansively.

'We don't make policy for our Council,' Charm said innocently. 'We're simple world-travellers. Our only involvement in this affair was discovering uninitiated world-travellers in Shattershard and attempting to teach them the customs of the Collegiate.'

'Don't listen to her,' Kal interrupted. 'Don't trust her. She can read your mind.'

He was determined to use every chance he had to save Morgan and he felt a rush of relief when Lisle Weft, the elderly female Jurist, met his eyes.

'This is not the first time I've heard suggestions that the Wheel is in breach of Collegiate codes,' she said, with a strange expression as she watched the twins. 'I suggest we send a couple of the Jurists with these two helpful young people, just to confirm that Morgan and Alex-Iskander reach their home safely.'

The twins exchanged glances but then to Kal's surprise Ciren said smoothly, 'We have no objection to that, your honour,' and Kal knew the brief chance to escape this trap was lost.

'I'm going with you too then,' he said, staring at the twins.

'I think not.' Dalandran's voice was sharp with command. 'I have no confidence that you wouldn't pursue some private vendetta against these people.'

'You have no authority over me!' Kal informed him. 'I'll go where I wish.' And, reflexively, his hand moved to his sword hilt.

As if from a great distance Kal heard Morgan gasp together with shouts around the room and saw Dalandran raise his hands in a warding gesture, directed at him. But before the Jurist's spell could take effect Kal felt the spikes of the Archon's crown tighten around his head and a feeling as if all his joints were freezing together at once. A flood of silver washed over his vision and he blacked out.

The attention of the observing crowds had shifted away from the group after the sentencing but people had turned back to watch as the argument got heated. Zoë had been uncomprehending, watching Morgan and Kal accusing the twins, and now she stared in amazement as Kal seemed to freeze in place, held as motionless as a statue, and his figure acquired a strange silver dazzle like sparks of static.

The two Jurists standing with Alex steered him across the room to join the twins as Ciren took hold of Morgan's unresisting arm. The black-haired Goth girl seemed numb with shock, staring at the frozen figure of the Archon with dumb horror.

'I can't believe this,' Alex muttered as Charm turned to him and gestured towards one of the room's exits. He looked back at Jhezra and then Laura with an expression of betrayal.

'Farewell, Alexander,' Jhezra said, her dark eyes moist with tears. 'I wish you well.'

'Goodbye, Alex,' Laura said calmly. 'Good luck with the A levels.' Then her head turned as she asked into space, 'So are you off back to Earth then, Zoë? I'm sure they'd take you if you asked.'

The identical twins turned two sets of purple-black eyes on Zoë like lasers and she blanched, stepping automatically closer to Jhezra. Pale pointed faces stared at her from white-blond helmets of hair.

'Who . . . what *are* you?' she couldn't help herself saying and the twins looked back expressionlessly.

'Ciren.'

'Charm.'

'Agents of the faction of the Wheel,' they finished together.

They waited but Zoë couldn't find anything to say and after a moment the twins released her from their attention. Two Jurists followed them as they led Morgan and Alex away.

The rest of the audience seemed to realize that the drama was over. Glossali Intergrade went up to Laura and touched her arm solicitously. From the Jurists' podium Dalandran stepped down and went over to Kal's motionless body and frowned at it. Around the room a couple of people were already mounting pulpits and beginning new speeches.

'I don't think much of Collegiate justice,' Zoë said, finally finding her voice, and Jhezra nodded grimly.

'Sometimes I have my doubts.' A dry female voice spoke from behind them and Zoë turned in surprise to see Lisle Weft looking grimly after the twins from the Wheel. 'I'm beginning to see that Caravaggion was right.'

'He was right?' Zoë repeated in confusion. 'About what? That it's pointless to give anyone any advice?'

But Lisle wasn't really listening to her. At her side the silky-haired red dog whined and Lisle nodded to herself.

'I think there's about to be a change in the weather,' she said.